A Drizzle of Magic

Related Titles by S. Usher Evans

The Weary Dragon Inn Series

Ale and Amnesia *(Newsletter Exclusive)*

Drinks and Sinkholes

Fiends and Festivals

Secrets and Snowflakes

Beasts and Baking

Magic and Molemen

Veils and Villains

Zealots and Zeniths

Campaigns and Curses

Perils and Potions

Royals and Ruses

Witch's Cove Series

A Mer-Murder at the Cove

S. USHER EVANS

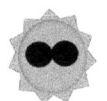

Sun's Golden Ray
Publishing

PENSACOLA, FL

Version Date: 11/11/24
© 2025 S. Usher Evans
ISBN: 978-1-965767-01-6
Retail Version

All rights reserved. No portion of this publication may be reproduced, stored in a retrieval system, or transmitted by any means—electronic, mechanical, photocopying, recording, or any other—except for brief quotations in printed reviews, without the prior written permission of the publisher.

Map created by CartographyBird
Cover Design and Chapter Typography by Sun's Golden Ray Publishing
Cupcake Line Art by Clara Fang
Line Editing by Danielle Fine, By Definition Editing

Sun's Golden Ray Publishing
Pensacola, FL
www.sgr-pub.com

For ordering information, please visit
www.sgr-pub.com/orders

To the
Kickstarters

CHAPTER ONE

"Perfect!"

Lillie Dean stared into the oven, eyeing the color and texture of the blueberry muffins baking away. It was opening day for her brand-new business, Pobyd Perfections Bakery, and she wanted *everything* to be as the bakery's name suggested. Already cooling and ready to be plated on the window ledge were several berry tartlets, a large apple pie, and a two-tiered cake that she'd finished icing and decorating. Next to those were a dozen strawberry cupcakes, an assortment of sugar-crusted wedding cookies, and blueberry scones.

Lillie had been up since the early morning hours working through her long to-do list of pastries. She'd wanted to catch the merchants and sailors who walked by every morning on their way to the docks at the end of Main Street. Many had stopped to peer inside as Lillie painted, gathered supplies, and built a beautiful decorative case to hold her baked goods.

Well, *she* hadn't built it. Earl Dollman—the lovely old carpenter who'd accompanied Lillie to Silverkeep along with his wife Etheldra—had done that for her. The couple had wanted to go on a first anniversary trip, but when they'd seen the state of Lillie's would-be bakery, both had insisted on staying and helping her get it shipshape. They'd continued on their trip the day before, and them leaving had been like saying goodbye to Pigsend all over again. If Lillie thought about it too much, she'd get too emotional. But there was far too much to do today, and she was eager to make the first day of her new bakery a good one. As a pobyd, a magical creature with the ability to make already delicious things even more so, she had poured all her love and excitement into the batter, as she had with everything else already baked. She was eager to show the citizens of Silverkeep exactly how much she appreciated them, and couldn't wait to show off what she'd made.

First, though, the muffins needed to cool. Lillie

put them down on her large kitchen table, which Earl had constructed with wood brought from Pigsend. There was still a faint smell of lacquer— he'd applied the final coat the night before— and Lillie could barely look at it without feeling overwhelmed with gratitude.

Sitting in the corner of the table was a jar full of flour dough—another gift from Pigsend. Lillie's dear friend Bev, the innkeeper at the Weary Dragon, had given her a bit of dough starter so Lillie could make Bev's famous rosemary bread. Not that she'd dream of selling it. No, that bread would be for her and her alone, a perennial reminder of the temporary home she'd grown to love.

The cupcakes weren't quite ready to be iced, so Lillie walked to the large window with the bakery's name painted on it. The sky had lightened significantly since she'd started baking, but the sun wasn't all the way up. Still, there were already dockhands on the street, lunch pails in hand, rubbing sleep out of their eyes as they went to work.

Lillie recognized one familiar face in the bunch, and hurried to catch her before she left for the day. Nikola Koven was a tiny thing, with wind-worn, tanned skin and hands that seemed perpetually calloused. But she had a kind smile and had been happy when Lillie moved in. She was a fisherfolk by trade, with a small dinghy that she used to bring in her catch which was sold by her husband Ursil at the market down the road.

"Morning, Nikola," Lillie called, stepping outside. "Lovely day, isn't it?"

"I thought I heard you moving about early this morning," Nikola said.

"Best time to bake," Lillie said. "I pulled a batch of muffins from the oven. Could I interest you in one?"

"I don't think sugar will agree with me this early," Nikola said, patting her stomach. "But maybe the mister will be by later. I told him at dinner last night that you'd moved in. He was—predictably—ecstatic."

"Tell him to come by," Lillie said. "I'm always eager for taste-testers. And he should tell his friends, too! We're officially open for business."

But Nikola was frowning at the window. "That's awfully brave of you, coming out with your name like that."

"What?" Lillie followed her gaze. "Pobyd Perfections? Why?" She waved Nikola off. "The queen's gone, remember? No need for us to live in fear anymore."

Nikola shook herself. "Well, it's your neck, I guess." With that, the fisherfolk walked away, muttering to herself.

Two months ago, Nikola would've been correct. Queen Meandra had been in control, and had outlawed every single type of magic there was. Even people with a spark of it were in danger of being arrested (or worse). But Lillie had it on good authority that Meandra had quite recently been overthrown, and all her prejudiced laws had gone with her.

But the news had taken a while to spread, and Lillie was still finding people who hadn't heard. Or worse, didn't believe it, like Nikola. The truth was the truth, though, and eventually, everyone would come to terms with the new normal.

Lillie walked up to the sign on her window and slid her nail along one of the letters to even it out. Then she smiled and walked back into her bakery.

At seven on the dot, Lillie propped the front door open. She'd realized too late that she didn't have a sign or any markings to denote the bakery was ready for business, but the sights and smells wafting from inside would be hard to miss.

At seven-thirty, Lillie piled blueberry muffins onto one of her plates and stood on the street, waving at passersby and smiling.

At eight, Lillie, who still hadn't sold a single thing, returned the plate to the window and adjusted the cakes. Everything certainly *looked* scrumptious. And there had been a slew of potential customers walking by all morning. Some had eyed the muffins with interest, but most had ignored her.

"Hmph."

Lillie wasn't one to be deterred. She tapped her foot on the ground and pursed her lips, debating her next move. It was very clear she needed better word-of-mouth advertising, which would be hard if no one actually stepped into the bakery. But she wasn't without friends...including one upstairs. In a few hours, Ursil would leave to sell the fish his wife had caught in the early morning hours. If he told the other merchants about Lillie's bakery being open, that might encourage a few of them to stop in.

She placed one blueberry muffin on a plate, along with a piece of decorative paper Etheldra had somehow managed to find for her. Then with a smile, she walked out the front door and up the stairs to the small landing. She'd met Nikola twice now but hadn't yet met her husband, and figured now was as good a time as any.

Lillie rapped on the door. "Mr. Koven? It's Lillie, your neighbor. I've brought you something sweet."

She waited a moment then rapped again. Nothing. Perhaps it was too early. Just as she was about to leave, telling herself she'd try again later, the door opened, and a disheveled Ursil appeared wearing a long pajama shirt. He was short, with watery eyes, round cheeks, and large ears, and looked very much like he'd just been rudely awoken.

"Whadya want?" he grumbled.

"Oh, I'm terribly sorry," Lillie said, her cheeks

heating. "Your wife, erm… She said you'd wanted to…" She swallowed her words. "Muffin?"

Ursil took the proffered pastry then turned and slammed the door.

Lillie winced. "Mr. Koven doesn't wake up before nine. Good to know."

She returned to the bakery, still slightly embarrassed but unwilling to give up. She once again stood in the doorway of the bakery, though this time, she opted for the strawberry cupcakes. They were made by reducing a pound of mashed strawberries and had a distinctive pink color (made more pink by Lillie's encouragement of the pink berry juice, of course).

But not only did no one come by, people were actively crossing the street to avoid talking with her.

"Well, goodness me." Lillie walked back inside. It was now nine-thirty, and besides the one muffin she'd given to Ursil upstairs, she hadn't sold a single pastry. Hadn't even *spoken* to anyone.

She placed the cupcakes back down in the front display case and put her hands on her hips, looking around. The bakery itself was quite inviting. She'd painted the walls a calming shade of light purple and added seafoam green accents. There were two sets of iron tables and chairs for potential patrons to sit and enjoy their food. The windows were bright and clean…

Pobyd Perfections Bakery

"That's *not* why," Lillie muttered to herself, brushing off Nikola's comment.

She paced the bakery a little longer, watching the clock. It wasn't as if she had a line out the door. She could close up shop for a bit and go for a walk, probably without missing a single customer.

With a determined smile on her face, Lillie boxed up an assortment of her goods, including several scones, muffins, tartlets, and a strawberry cupcake. Then she locked the front door to the bakery, making sure everything was good and secure before heading up the street.

Going from the bakery to the town square wasn't exactly a stroll. Her bakery was nestled at the bottom of the rather steep hill that ran the length of the town. While the town square wasn't far, the incline was enough for Lillie's calves to start aching before she'd passed the first block.

Still, she wore a smile as she approached the town hall. It was a beautiful building, made of white brick and featuring a large clock tower. Beneath the tower was a staircase that led to a pair of wooden doors, which Lillie pushed open with her elbow. Inside, there were rows of benches for a town meeting, as well as offices for the mayor, whom Lillie had yet to meet, as well as for Mr. Abora, the assistant mayor, and Sheriff Arelia Juno.

Mr. Abora wasn't in, but the sheriff was. She was

a stout woman who didn't seem ruffled by most things. When Lillie met her, she'd been wearing a queenspin, but she'd now lost it. Maybe the news *had* started spreading about the queen's defeat.

"Good morning, Ms. Dean," Juno said with a thin smile. "Is there something I can help you with?"

"Oh, no. I thought I'd come by with some goodies," Lillie said, showing off the box. "A thank you for all the help Mr. Abora's given me."

"Kemp will be in shortly, I'm sure." She went back to scribbling on paper.

"Right." Lillie shifted awkwardly. "Well, then. Suppose I'll wait for him."

Lillie sat on one of the benches and craned her neck to look around. It was similar in shape and size to the Pigsend town hall, with two sets of benches bifurcated by a single walkway in the middle. At the front of the room was a small table and a single chair, which Lillie imagined was where the mayor sat during town meetings. Were they as contentious as back in Pigsend? Lillie hoped not.

The door opened, and Mr. Abora breezed in, looking harried. He was a tall, thin man with long black hair braided down his back which had several strands out of place. His eyes were glued to a stack of papers in his hand, and he barely noticed Lillie as she called his name. When she said it again, panic flashed on his face.

"Oh, it's you," he said with a sigh. "Good morning."

"Good morning. I brought you some pastries," Lillie said. "I opened my doors today and thought it would be nice to bring you a thank you."

His shoulders drooped, and he beckoned her to follow him inside. He tossed his bag on the floor and began rifling through paperwork.

"Are you all right?" Lillie asked.

"No, I was bombarded on my way in this morning by Reed Norwood—he's a merchant who owns a townhouse up on the north end of town." He sighed as Sheriff Juno popped out of her office. "Apparently, there was a prowler in his house the night before. Someone came right up to his bedroom, woke him up, then disappeared."

"That's awful!" Lillie gasped, putting her hands to her mouth. She'd thought Silverkeep was a safe town.

"Well, the prowler was still there this morning," Kemp said. "Apparently, it's Jim Clench—he owned that townhouse before the war and was trying to get back into his home. Now he's up in arms because he says someone's squatting on his property."

"I'll take care of it," Sheriff Juno muttered, getting to her feet and walking out. "Again."

"Fifth incident like that this week," Mr. Abora said with a sigh. "People wanting to know why they no longer have shops or townhouses and when the *squatters* are going to leave. Like those people haven't been living there for six years."

"Goodness, what a mess," Lillie said. "You don't think…is someone going to come back for the bakery, do you think?"

"Well, it wasn't a bakery before," he said. "But that whole stretch of Main Street had been somewhat abandoned even before the war." He sighed. "Of course, if someone shows up, demanding—"

"I'll be sure to bring it to your attention," Lillie said.

He let out a breath, finally noticing the box of sweets. "What's that?"

"Just a little sweet something to brighten your day," Lillie said, pushing the box over to him. "Clearly, you can use it."

To Lillie's delight, he sank into his chair and smiled as he plucked a scone from the box and took a hearty bite. Predictably, he sat right back up in excitement.

"Goodness me, Ms. Dean," he said, swallowing the bite. "You're quite the baker. This might be the most delicious scone I've ever had in my life."

Lillie beamed. "I'm so glad you like it."

"Do you have more? Maybe I can bring them over to Mr. Norwood's house. Maybe something sweet will lighten everyone's mood."

"You know," Lillie said slowly. "If you need

some sweets with a bit of...encouragement, I can do that."

He frowned. "What do you mean?"

"I'm a pobyd," Lillie said. "That means I make delicious things, but I can also add different suggestions to my baked goods. Maybe I can whip up a dozen cupcakes with the intention to get along and solve problems."

He stared at her as if she had two heads. "You're a...pobyd?"

"Y-yes?" Lillie said, realizing too late that Mr. Abora *didn't* know that about her. She'd obviously hidden it in Pigsend when the queen had been in power, but the topic hadn't come up since she'd moved to Silverkeep.

"How did you escape the queen's..." He cleared his throat. "The queen's people? I know there were soldiers in Pigsend. I saw them."

Lillie shifted. She wasn't comfortable telling the *whole* story about the six years she'd been in hiding, especially the parts about Lower Pigsend. "Luck and keeping my head down. There were a few close calls, too, but..."

But thanks to Bev, Lillie had avoided any major consequences. It was more than she deserved, and she was keen on paying her good fortune forward.

"I don't think... I didn't..." He cleared his throat. "Well, you're here now. And if the rumors are true, the queen's defeated, so... we won't have to worry about her, will we?"

"Hopefully not," Lillie said.

The front doors opened, and a pair of loudly arguing men came storming in, followed by Sheriff Juno. "Goodness, I've got to sort this. Thank you for the scone, Ms. Dean! I appreciate it." He slid the box back to her. "Feel free to take this with you."

Lillie rose, waiting a moment to watch the argument before deciding it wasn't her business.

Chapter Two

Lillie walked out of the town hall and stood on the front steps, looking around. Every building on the square held some kind of shop or merchant office. To her immediate left, a cobbler, a seamstress, a milliner, and a candlemaker all sat in narrow buildings along one block. The next block held a butcher, a rope maker, and one of three ornate offices for a merchant. The other two were catty-corner, joined by a glassblower in the third building. Then the Globe Café, the Silverkeep Inn, the town hall, and a small schoolhouse. Earl had said Gilda Climber's forge was around the corner from the café and had an entire block to itself. Lillie made a mental note to visit the other Pigsend transplant soon.

She held the box and considered her options. She didn't know much about the Globe Café, which, from its sign, seemed to sell coffee. She did see one or two customers in the outside seating area with small plates, so it was possible they sold baked goods, too.

Next to that was the Silverkeep Inn, where Lillie had stayed several nights. The innkeeper, Noemi Lyle, had been pleasant, though not quite friendly. Still, there hadn't been any sort of breakfast offered, which might be an opportunity. Back in Pigsend, Lillie had brought pastries to the Weary Dragon every morning, so maybe she could strike a similar deal in Silverkeep.

She approached the two-level building with her shoulders back and a smile on her face. Inside the dark, wood-covered space, there were four round tables around the front room, with a stone-covered hearth. Tapestries on the walls depicted scenes from sea battles of yesteryear, and an inset area to the back stored barrels of ale that would be served with dinner. Next to that was a long table where the innkeeper served her dinners, and, perhaps, where she'd serve Lillie's pastries in the mornings.

"Ms. Lyle?" Lillie called. "It's Lillie Dean. Are you around?"

"Back here."

Lillie followed the voice, finding Noemi in the small back yard, surrounded on both sides by other buildings. It was awfully cramped, and even Noemi's vegetable garden looked like it missed open space. The innkeeper was kneeling over a bucket and scrubbing sheets. She had dark curly hair and pale skin tanned darker from being out in the sun.

"Settled in all right at your bakery?" she asked, dunking the washing. "Your friends left early this morning."

Lillie nodded. "I do hope Etheldra wasn't too blunt for you. She does have a good heart, but her delivery can be a bit—"

"I've dealt with worse." The innkeeper pulled the sheets out. "What can I do for you?"

"Oh, well." Lillie opened the pastry box. "Hungry?"

Noemi didn't look up at her. "Bit busy at the moment."

Lillie snapped the box shut. "Right. Of course you are. Um." She swallowed her unease. "I was thinking it might be nice for your guests to get a pastry or two in the morning before they leave."

"For free?" she said with an eyebrow raise.

"Well, erm, yes," Lillie said. "Back where I'm from—"

"Pigsend."

"Yes, Pigsend. The Weary Dragon's owner had

an agreement with our bakery. She paid us a gold a week, and we brought over a basket of muffins or tartlets or whatever we were making for the tea shop. The guests got a sweet send-off, and the innkeeper didn't have to fuss with breakfast."

"I already don't fuss with breakfast," she said, dunking another set of sheets into the water. "And a gold per week is a lot of money."

Lillie held her breath, waiting for more, but the only sound was the sloshing of the water. "I...see..." She swallowed her disappointment. "Well, if you change your mind, you know where to find me."

"Business can't be *that* bad that you're already trying to outsource it," Ms. Lyle said, eyeing her. "Hasn't Mr. Kemp given you a large sum of gold to start?"

"He has," Lillie said. "Just trying to be proactive and make solid partnerships. The bakery business can be a bit up and down, you know. Nice to have some reliable income." Lillie toyed with the cover on the box, waiting for the innkeeper to speak again. When she didn't, she said, "Well, thank you for your time. I'll leave you to your laundry."

~

Lillie returned to the bakery and propped the door open again, hoping the scents and smells would entice people to come in. She busied herself first with reorganizing the display window then writing down some ideas for what to bake next based on the ingredients she had. She wasn't panicking yet, but it was wise to be intentional about buying more ingredients.

The hours ticked on, and Lillie stood in the doorway, holding a plate of cupcakes and calling out to the passersby, noticing with a frown that they *were* eyeing the name of the bakery. She fretted a moment—had she been too hasty in the name?—then dismissed it. There was *nothing* to be ashamed of. Before the war, pobyds had been hired in kitchens and bakeries all over the place. There'd even been one serving the king, if rumors were to be believed. Lillie had worked in bakeries in Sheepsburg before the war broke out, and after, she'd started her own bakery in Lower Pigsend, where no one had thought twice about buying from a pobyd.

But the flash of concern in Mr. Abora's eyes had been unmistakable, as had the worry on Nikola's. It was entirely possible—realistic, even—that the people of Silverkeep, after years of living in fear of anything magical, wouldn't be quick to patronize a bakery using it so obviously. So she'd have to keep at it, and perhaps ration her flour a little better.

At the end of her first day, Lillie had sold exactly zero pastries, but she did her best not to take it personally. The goods would still be okay to sell tomorrow after a quick spell to infuse life back into them. Although they would've been better the day they were made, a layman wouldn't be able to tell the difference. Wearily, she climbed the stairs to her small apartment, which was a single room containing a bed, a kitchenette with a tiny wood-burning stove, and a rocking chair. She'd been so busy baking that she hadn't started a loaf of bread earlier in the day to eat with dinner, so she had to settle for a blueberry scone with a few slices of cheese. She fixed herself a cup of tea, courtesy of Etheldra, and cozied up with a knitted blanket made by Merv, a six-foot moleman who loved to knit.

She glanced at a stack of paper on the small table next to her. Bev had made Lillie promise she'd write, and Lillie had hoped to pen a note with tales of bakery lines out the door and lots of new friends. Writing a forlorn note about an empty shop and baked goods gone stale wasn't the sort of update she wanted to send.

"I promise I'll write when there's good news," Lillie said. "And there *will* be good news. Tomorrow will be better. It has to be."

The next morning, Lillie woke up at four to make a new batch of muffins and cast a freshening spell on all the pastries she'd baked the day before. It was one of the most useful spells she had, where she suggested to the flour that it might absorb a bit of the water hanging nearby and take more of the sun's heat to keep warm. But even a pobyd had her limits, and if Lillie didn't move the pastries in the window today, tossing them might be the better option.

She paced the front room, talking to herself. The Silverkeep Inn was out, but that didn't mean all her options were out. The Globe Café could be an option. After all, Mr. Abora had expressly invited her *because* there wasn't another baker in town. It was entirely possible he'd wanted her to meet with the Globes and offer her services. Mr. Globe was her landlord, and presumably, he also owned the café, too. Mr. Abora had probably been so busy dealing with the returned folks that he hadn't had time to make introductions.

"Yes, I'm sure that's it," Lillie said, almost convincing herself it was true.

When Lillie looked out the window and saw the steady stream of people avoiding her shop had slowed, she locked up and carried another box of delicious sweets up the road. She'd rehearsed what she might say to the owner, who might or might not be her landlord, hoping he wouldn't notice that she was offering yesterday's goods.

But as she walked up to the café, which was a nice, white brick building with a large awning hanging over the alley next door to offer more outdoor seating, Lillie's stomach dropped. There were tartlets and muffins alongside the cups of coffee, and as she peered in *this* window, she spotted a display case, not unlike hers, filled with pastries.

"Oh, no..." she muttered, looking down at her box of pastries.

This *perhaps* explained why no one had wanted to come to her bakery.

She stashed her box of pastries behind a bush and walked up to a couple eating under the awning.

"Excuse me," Lillie said. "How long has this café been here?"

"Oh, hm?" The round-faced woman frowned at her partner. "I think it's been a year, right?"

The tall, thin woman nodded. "About a year, yes."

"Thank you," Lillie said, her stomach clenching.

She left the two women and approached the café, full of nerves. It had been here a year? So that meant... But Lillie had reached out to Mr. Abora and *asked* if the offer was still open, and he'd said yes. So he'd invited her to come when he knew there was already a baker in town?

"Don't panic, Lillie," she muttered, pushing open the door. "Just figure out what's going on."

Inside, the scent of coffee was overwhelming, along with the faint aroma of flour, yeast, butter, and sugar. There were more tables, too, which were fuller than the ones outside. The floor was black-and-white checkerboard, and the display case seemed much larger and nicer than the one in Lillie's shop—and there was a line of waiting customers. Behind the counter, two young attendants moved quickly between the carafes of coffee and the pastry case.

Lillie joined the queue, her stomach turning on itself, and watched as the exact same pastries she'd baked the day before were served to customers.

When she reached the front of the line, she was practically sick with worry and almost didn't hear the nasal voice of the attendant.

"I said, what do you want?" the girl repeated, sounding quite impatient. She couldn't have been older than fifteen and clearly wanted to be anywhere but here.

"Oh, um…" Lillie inspected the bakery case again, earning a sigh from the girl. "Can I have one of those tartlets? And I suppose I'll try a coffee, too."

"How do you want your coffee?" She looked bored as she reached down, yanked one of the tartlets out, and slammed it onto a small plate on the counter.

"Erm, I'm not sure I know how to answer that," Lillie said. "However you like it, I suppose."

"I hate coffee."

"Then however most people get it," Lillie tried again.

The girl rolled her eyes and walked to a large carafe in the corner. She poured dark brown, hot liquid into a cup, set the cup on a saucer, and placed it next to the tartlet.

"Anything else?"

"Just a question," Lillie said. "Who makes all these pastries?"

She clicked her tongue. "That would be Mr. Globe." She paused, perhaps reading Lillie's surprised face. "Not *that* Mr. Globe. That's big Mr. Globe, who owns the town. The baker here is Julian Globe, his son." She paused. "I think he actually owns this place, too. Julian, not Mr. Globe."

Lillie relaxed, a little. "I haven't met either Mr. Globe yet."

"You don't wanna," she said.

"Why not?" Lillie said. "Mr. Globe—the elder one—is my landlord, I believe. He's been quite kind to me, inviting me to come to town and—"

"You and everyone else," she said, exasperated. "Can I get you anything else? There's a line."

Lillie paid the girl then gingerly took her cup and pastry to a somewhat hidden table in the corner. Luckily, no one seemed to give her a second glance. She settled into the wrought-iron chair and picked up the tartlet to inspect it. The crust seemed dry and not at all flaky. When she turned it over, the filling had seeped through to the bottom, making that part soggy and not at all appealing. The cream filling had almost scrambled instead of emulsified, as if they'd added the eggs to a too-hot mixture. The fruit on top, at least, looked edible, but that was the only positive thing she could say about the whole thing.

"Maybe it tastes better than it looks," she said

with a sigh.

But when she bit into it, she found it every bit as lackluster as she'd been expecting. With some difficulty, she swallowed the first bite. When she gulped the coffee to wash it down, she found it bitter and almost undrinkable. She coughed, her eyes watering, and had to breathe with her hand over her mouth for a moment to keep from being sick.

"Well, no one *asked* you to eat it."

Lillie jumped, looking up into the disgruntled, angry face of a tall man with black hair and broad shoulders. If he hadn't been scowling at her, he might've actually been striking, with his deep brown skin and sharp cheekbones. But Lillie noticed too late that he wore an apron covered in flour and smears of chocolate, and that he'd *probably* had spent a lot of time on the item she'd spat out.

"Mr...Globe?" Lillie scrambled to her feet. "I'm so sorry. My name is Lillie Dean, and—"

"I know who you are," he said, crossing his arms over his chest. "But what I don't know is what gave you the idea that you could come into my shop and insult me like this?"

Chapter Three

Lillie swallowed hard, scrambling to think of a reason to be in here that wouldn't set him off. She couldn't possibly tell him she'd come hoping to partner with him, only to find he already had pastries for sale *then* discovered they were absolutely inedible. No, that certainly wouldn't go over well.

"I...wanted to...introduce myself," she said, after a moment's thought. "I saw the name and I thought you might be...my landlord?"

"No," he snarled. "That's my *father*. I'm Julian Globe."

"Ah." Lillie wiped her hands on her shirt and

held out her hand. "Well, I'm pleased to make your acquaintance, Julian."

"I'm not." His eyes narrowed to slits. "You're an unwelcome invader."

"I don't think I'm *unwelcome*," Lillie said, coming to her feet. "Mr. Abora invited me—"

"That clown." Julian scoffed and uncrossed his arms then crossed them over his chest again. "Sticking his nose where it doesn't belong. *Obviously*, we don't need a baker here."

Don't you, though? Lillie swallowed that thought and plastered on a smile. "Now, I think we've gotten off on the wrong foot." She held out her hand again. "I'm not your enemy."

"You're here to scope out the competition," he said. "Tasting my goods. I hope you paid for them."

"I did, actually. You can ask your…lovely clerk," Lillie said, nodding to the younger of the two girls. "And I'm not your competition. Or at least, I don't want to be." She gestured to the coffee. "I'm not serving that, in any case."

"And why not?" Julian, who seemed bound and determined to argue with everything Lillie said, flexed his arms aggressively. "Our coffee is renowned in this region. We're the only ones who can get it. Have an exclusive deal with a merchant across the sea who'll sell only to us."

Perhaps because no one else can stomach the stuff. "My point is that our businesses are different enough that they can coexist."

"Well, you can *coexist* elsewhere," he said, pointing to the door. "If I see you here again—"

"You won't," Lillie said, hearing the message loud and clear. "Have a good day, Mr. Globe."

Lillie hastily made her escape, feeling the eyes of every person in the bakery on her. Well, at least they'd overheard their conversation and might be curious enough to stop in. Julian really was a sour man—though with his deep brown eyes and well-sculpted features, he might actually be handsome if he stopped *scowling* like a child. She glanced back at the confections in the window. His anger toward her came probably from a place of real concern, though. After all, if that was what he was passing off as pastries, she really wouldn't have to work hard to steal his business.

Once people actually came *inside* her shop, that was.

She stood in the square, glancing at the town hall directly across from her, then at the other stores on the square. Everyone on the street was watching her, as if they'd overheard the exchange between her and Julian. She lifted her chin, eager to move on and find her customers elsewhere.

But she'd only taken two steps before she ran into someone and fell backward onto her rear. "Oof!"

"Lillie Dean?"

Lillie started and looked up, shock turning into dread as the other person's face came into view. "B-Benetta?"

The other woman made no move to help Lillie get up, so she scrambled to her feet herself. "W-what are you doing here?"

"I could ask you the same question." Benetta was the same height as Lillie but wore several bustles under her skirt that gave her a bigger presence. She had pointed ears and purple spots along her forehead, though the spots were covered by a layer of face paint. The ears, though, were out for everyone to see. She'd lived in the same neighborhood as Lillie in Lower Pigsend and was a seamstress by trade.

"Oh, I..." Lillie cleared her throat. "I'm... I live here now. Why are you here?"

"I'm *from* here," she said purposefully. "Back in town to reclaim my property and the business I had to abandon." She eyed Lillie. "I'd heard there was a pobyd in town, but I can't believe it's... Well, I daresay I never thought I'd see you again after the *incident*."

Lillie put her hands on her hips, her cheeks flushing. "You know, nothing *happened*. The spell was never broken. The talisman never left the confines of Lower Pigsend."

"It's enough that *you* thought you could steal it

for your own selfish gains," Benetta said. "Do you think you're the only one who missed the sun? Missed real food?" She scoffed. "The rest of us lived with it because *we knew what would happen otherwise.*"

Lillie swallowed. Nothing Benetta said was untrue. Lower Pigsend had been safe from the queen, but due to its underground location and needing to be completely closed off from the rest of the world, fresh food was hard to come by. Lillie had been without wheat flour or fresh fruits, and the only vegetables she could bake with were those they could grow underground, like carrots, beets, and potatoes. In a fit of desperation, Lillie had stolen the protective talisman keeping the enclave hidden, believing the wizard Percival would simply recast the protections she'd broken and everyone had been safe. But Percival had been quite ill (unknown to everyone in town), and thankfully, Lillie had been thwarted before any major damage had been done. She'd then been kicked out of the underground haven permanently.

Lillie had left Lower Pigsend with nothing but the clothes on her back, so Bev had taken pity on her then, offering her a room at the Weary Dragon and introducing her to Allen Mackey, the baker next door with a spark of pobyd in his blood. While working together to expand his business, Lillie had taught Allen how to use and control his magic.

She'd also helped Bev detangle several mysteries, one by baking some truth-telling bread for an election. Lillie had hoped helping her new friends would erase the guilt for the danger she'd put the citizens of Lower Pigsend in, but it lingered. The past always seemed ready to catch up with her.

Now, perhaps, her chickens had finally come home to roost.

"I'm not proud of what I did," Lillie said, after a long pause. "And I was punished for it."

"Not enough," Benetta sneered. "If you ask me, you should've been handed over to the queen's people for the chaos you nearly caused."

Lillie swallowed hard. She nearly *had* been.

"And now you expect to keep living your life as if you hadn't endangered all of ours?" Benetta said. "Are you one of the miscreants who stole property that didn't belong to them?"

"I was invited here by Mr. Abora," Lillie said softly.

"Yes, I've got words for *him*, too." Benetta picked up her sizable skirts and glared at the town hall. "Because if he thinks he can *give away* property owned by six generations of *my* family, he's got another think coming!"

Lillie watched her go, feeling like the wind had been knocked out of her twice in ten minutes. First, finding the café wasn't only a coffee shop but a bakery (though the head baker didn't seem able to make a decent custard), and now there was someone in Silverkeep who could tell everyone about Lillie's awful mistake...

"Just because she can, doesn't mean she will," Lillie whispered, turning to head back to the bakery. But the optimism with which Lillie had started the day vanished.

The sun continued to cross the sky slowly, and the shop remained empty, save one nervous pobyd. As the reflections on the houses turned orange, Lillie had to admit she might be in trouble—especially as she pulled all the two-day-old pastries to throw away. She absolutely *hated* pitching her hard work and hated losing money even more. But as she tasted one of the scones, she grimaced. It wasn't awful, but it wasn't up to the Pobyd Perfections standard. Whatever that was.

"What would Bev do?" Lillie muttered to herself as she looked around her shop. The mysterious innkeeper *always* had a handle on things, even when the world was falling apart. Lillie wished for a tenth of Bev's even-keeled temperament.

Bev would make rosemary bread, that was what she'd do.

Not that it would solve any of Lillie's problems, but at least it would make her think of home. Bev started her famous bread using leftover dough from the night before, and she'd given Lillie some in a jar to take with her. Lillie had made the bread while Bev had been elsewhere (perhaps defeating the queen? Lillie still wasn't sure of her role in things), and had the recipe down by heart now. She assembled the ingredients, including the dough, flour, salt, and water, and a few sprigs of rosemary she'd brought from Bev's garden, and mixed them together until they resembled a shaggy mess. She let that sit while she inspected her stores, and thought about what she might bake tomorrow morning to replace all she'd thrown away. She had a crate of strawberries and more blueberries, but she'd have to find that farmers' market to get eggs and milk.

After an hour, the dough had absorbed the water, and Lillie did the first set of stretches and folds then headed upstairs to fetch her dried meat and cheese from upstairs. There wasn't much left, so those would be also on her list of things to find tomorrow at the market. She sat at the kitchen table, eating and considering her next move, and reliving the two very rude conversations earlier.

She had some sympathy for Julian, but there really wasn't any need to be so nasty to her. Clearly, his business was thriving, and Lillie didn't pose any danger to him. There must've been something else behind his disdain, but it wasn't worth it to figure out what it was. She'd keep to her side of town, and he'd keep to his, and they'd be fine.

Benetta, though…Lillie couldn't shake her angst

about that. Not what she'd said, but what she threatened. The town already seemed leery about the new pobyd living there openly. What would they think if they found out she was a villain, too?

She finished her dinner then returned to the bread to stretch and fold it again, memories of watching the Weary Dragon innkeeper work her dough bubbling to the surface. Bev had thought Lillie was worth redeeming, so that must've made it true. Merv, too, had readily forgiven Lillie for her subterfuge, as long as Lillie continued bringing him sweets.

She smiled as she thought of her dear friends in Pigsend, and for the first time, felt a twinge of regret. Why *had* she been so keen to leave? She'd had everything she could ever want, although there were times at the bakery where it seemed there were more bakers than orders. And she'd liked living with her roommate Wilda, though the other woman had made it clear she expected help with her pies for the Harvest Festival. But Lillie knew everyone, and everyone at least liked her.

She couldn't even say the same for—

The front door opened. "Hello?"

Lillie jumped up, wiping her hands hastily, and dashed out, remembering too late she hadn't locked the door. "Can I—Oh, Mr. Koven!"

Lillie's neighbor stood in the front room, holding a hat and looking much less grumpy than he had the last time she'd seen him. He also smelled quite putrid, even from this distance, and Lillie had to assume he'd been gutting fish all day. Still, she needed to be neighborly, so she held her breath and approached.

"How's business?" he asked, looking somewhat awkward.

"Oh, well, um..." She let out a nervous laugh. "Terrible, actually. Haven't had a single customer."

"Really?" He frowned. "Why's that? Everythin' looks good enough to..." He glanced at the front case. "Oh. Wait. Where'd those muffins go?"

"They're in the back," Lillie said, thumbing toward the kitchen. "Can't sell them tomorrow, so I have to pitch them."

"No!" He stepped forward, his eyes wide. "Those were the best muffins I ever ate in my life! You can't toss 'em. I'll buy the lot. Don't care if they're a little stale." He reached into his pocket and brandished a gold coin then slammed it on the counter. "Throwin' them out, you gotta be off your rocker..."

Lillie smiled and ducked into the kitchen to grab the tray. "Here."

He snatched one and gobbled it down before she could say another word, letting out a sigh. "I swear, I don't know what you put in this, but I'm gonna eat this whole pan. Can't believe no one's been by. I been tryin', but every time I come by, you're not here."

"W-what?" Lillie frowned. "What do you mean?"

"Well, the missus goes out to fish early in the mornin', you know," he said, pointing toward his apartment. "I get a bit of a lie-in. I leave around ten or so to gut all the fish she's caught and sell 'em." He thumbed toward the outside. "Don't get home until now." He tilted his cap up. "But you've been closed the past two mornings when I leave for the market. That's probably why you're not sellin' anythin'. Gotta stay open for customers."

Lillie swallowed her excuses and arguments. "You're quite right. I do apologize for that. I was… running errands. Thought it would be safe to leave, but I suppose not." She picked up the gold coin he'd placed on the counter, smiling at her first bit of Silverkeep money. "You don't know what this means to me."

"You don't know what this means to *me*," Ursil said, now on his third muffin. "The missus can catch and cook a fish like you wouldn't believe, but baker, she is not. These smells were drivin' me batty." He cleared his throat. "I do apologize for being gruff with you the other day. Not much of a mornin' person."

"For a gold, you can be gruff with me all you want," Lillie said. "You said you sell fish at the market? The one on the wharf?"

He nodded. "Yeah, why?"

"That's the same one where you can get milk and eggs and produce, right?" Lillie asked, looking at the gold coin.

"It's a big market, but there's a section for all that, yeah," he said. "Why? You need some stuff?"

She nodded.

"Then you should bring a box of muffins, too," he said, chowing down on his fourth one. "I got loads of friends down there. Fishmongers, but farmers and the like, too. Everyone would be excited to hear there's a baker down the road."

"Really?" Lillie couldn't believe she hadn't been down to the market yet. But she *had* only been open two days. "And they won't... Well, I've been told my presence isn't exactly welcome."

"Why? Cause you're a perrbod?"

"Pobyd," Lillie corrected lightly. "And I think that's part of it. I found out today that Julian Globe, the café owner, was furious at my arrival. I think he'd rather see me on a wagon back to Pigsend."

"Bah. The Globes." He waved her off. "Bunch of rich snobs, if you ask me. They ain't ever got anythin' for us wharf folks, you know?" He grinned. "Probably Mr. Abora was thinkin' us lower folks could use something sweet so we'd keep bringin' all the goods that make the merchants wealthy. That's why he put you right around the corner from the fish market." He snapped his fingers. "How about this—I'll come getcha in the mornin' on my way in. Show you around, introduce you to everyone. If you've got ol' Ursil Koven's stamp of approval, you'll be in good company."

Lillie could've jumped over the counter and kissed the man. "What do you think they'd like? Scones? Muffins? Cupcakes?" She tapped her finger against her chin. "You know, Allen—my dear friend from back home—he used to make these delicious breakfast biscuits with meat and cheese. I could whip some of those up?"

"Bring 'em all. If they're half as good as that muffin, I daresay you'll sell out in minutes." He flashed another smile. "See you in the mornin'. Just erm…not too early."

Chapter Four

As she rose at four to begin baking, Lillie felt more hope than she had in days. She hummed to herself as she fired up the oven, shaped her rosemary bread (which had been proofing all night) then started on her confections for the day. She'd stayed up a little *too* late trying to think of her best pastries. Since it sounded like the fisherfolk already had a meal of dried meat and cheese, she'd forego the breakfast biscuits for now. Instead, she whipped up some more blueberry scones with a drizzle of sweet icing, along with cinnamon muffins. She tasted one of her strawberry cupcakes—she'd decided against throwing them away, after all. They were a bit on the off side, but passable.

When the early morning came and went without any customers, she didn't feel quite the same trepidation, but she still worried maybe Ursil had oversold his sway. Or perhaps there weren't that many fisherfolk down there. Or maybe no one actually liked sweets like he did.

But when her kindly neighbor walked in at a little after ten, as she was pulling the rosemary bread out of the oven, he was all smiles as he inhaled the scents. "I told the missus I couldn't believe our luck. A baker downstairs! I get to wake up to all these great smells." He sauntered over to the three boxes Lillie had packed up to bring to the market. "What do we have this mornin'?"

Lillie opened one of the boxes and named each pastry inside. He snatched a blueberry scone from the bunch and sighed as he savored it.

"Gonna spoil me, Miss Lillie." He shook his head.

"Lillie is fine," she said, picking up the other two boxes and walking with him out the door, pausing only to lock up. "If Ursil is all right with you?"

"Of course! We ain't that fancy around here," he said, nodding to the box in his arms. "Havin' a baker in our midst is going to be quite the change."

"I'm sure…" She considered her phrasing. "I'm

sure Globe Café had been doing an adequate job of satisfying Silverkeep's sweet tooth."

Ursil snorted. "You ain't been here long, but you're gonna find out pretty quick there's a divide in Silverkeep. The merchants and rich folk live around the square and the north end of town, away from the stink of the ocean and fish. They don't like to come down here—prefer to send their servants and maids and whatnots to get their supplies. And we southern-dwellin' folk get the hint when we try to venture up for a cup of tea or to get our clothes mended."

"Oh, I see." Lillie frowned. Mr. Abora certainly hadn't mentioned *that* when he'd given her this location. "Was it always like this?"

"From what I understand, yeah," he said. "The rich folks lived around the square. Poor folks down here. Then the whole town disappeared, practically, and those who were left decided to become rich. Or were invited to be by Mr. Abora. Once the square had all the right shops and people, the invitations stopped. Mr. Globe had all he needed again, and the rest of us could suffer."

"Is Mr. Globe your landlord, too?" Lillie asked. "The elder one, I mean."

"He's *everybody's* landlord. From what I understand, he was one of the only people left in town when the queen came through," he said. "Had enough money and the land was cheap enough with everyone gone that he put his name on every shop, office, and apartment in the city, just about. Then he set Mr. Abora to fillin' the place with paying tenants." He snorted. "It's a racket, if you ask me."

The wharf was much busier than it looked from the bakery's vantage point. It spanned the length of three blocks in either direction, with long wooden docks going far out into the water to meet the ships that came and went. Dockhands moved crates on and off ships as quickly as the hulls reached the slips, pausing only to argue and cajole each other.

"Where do all the ships come from?" Lillie asked, taking a moment to stand and watch the activity. "And what do they bring?"

"Ships come from all over," Ursil said. "They never stay long, though, because we ain't a major city or connected to a big river. We're quite a small port, really. Mostly we load up textiles and whatnot. Got a slew of cotton and wool farmers north of here."

Lillie couldn't imagine what a *larger* port would look like. "Julian said he gets his coffee beans shipped here from far away."

"Aye. Another perk of his father's connections. I sometimes think the only reason Julian Globe was allowed to open his café was so his father would have somewhere to sell that acrid concoction."

She smiled. "Not a fan?"

"Bah. Tastes like burnt firewood."

She'd thought the same. "I'm sure it's an acquired taste. If Julian would let me, I'd be happy to help him. I'm sure I could lessen the burnt flavor, and goodness knows I could help him with his pastry crusts and fillings." She stopped, realizing she might've been speaking too frankly. "If he was interested, of course. But it seems he's doing fine, as is."

Ursil cracked a grin. "I like you, Lillie. You ain't afraid to speak your mind."

The market took up two city blocks to the east, so they turned toward the left. Tables sat beneath off-white tents that lined both sides of the wharf, displaying everything from every color fish imaginable to crabs that snapped their pincers into the air and prawns and smaller crustaceans without heads.

But it wasn't only seafood for sale. As Lillie took in each of the nearby booths, three farmers had vegetables, a small woman with dark braids was reading a book at a table with several jugs of milk and crates of eggs, an old man was weaving rugs from brightly colored yarn, and a young girl sat under a tent filled with all manner of flowers.

There were far more people than Lillie had expected milling around, inspecting the products and chatting with the vendors. The stench of fish was more potent here, and it made Lillie's nose twitch. But Ursil didn't seem to mind, chattering away about life in Silverkeep as they wandered the stalls.

"Yeah, there's a whole dock out at the end of the market where the smaller boats get kept. The missus's boat is there, too, but there's at least twenty. They sail out into the open ocean and look for fish then bring it back to us to sell."

"Who do you sell it to if no one—?" Lillie stopped herself. "Right, you said the servants and maids come down for the rich folk, right?"

He nodded. "Fish is a big part of our diet here in the south. The rich folk get their cows and pigs and whatnot, but even they can't say no to a deliciously spicy grilled fillet." He licked his lips. "What's your favorite kind of fish?"

"I don't think I have one," Lillie said. "You'll have to show me what's good."

"That, I can do. Best fish comes from the missus's nets, of course. And here she comes now." He waved at Nikola, who was walking up to them carrying a large, dripping bag over her shoulder. She was drenched from the waist down, and her salt-and-pepper hair was windswept. Ursil handed Lillie the boxes he'd been carrying then ran up to take the bag from Nikola, pecking her lovingly on the cheek before dragging it behind an empty table.

"Where did you find those red fish?" a nearby fishmonger asked Nikola, his hand on his hip. "I haven't seen a school of them in weeks."

"Now, why would I tell you when I can get a silver per pound of fish, Jarvis?" Nikola replied with a look. "Maybe even per half pound, if the folks up north are hungry enough for it."

The fisherman growled and turned back to his own stall.

"Ah, I see Ursil finally caught up with you," Nikola said with a smile as she turned her attention back to Lillie and the boxes she carried. "And he's convinced you to bring your wares here."

"Y-yes, this is truly something else," Lillie said, glancing at the milk and egg farmer who was reading a book. "Ursil, that lovely young woman over there should be a friend of mine. Will you introduce us?"

"Oh, right!" Ursil looked at Nikola with a pleading expression. "Dearest Nik, would you—"

"Fine, fine," Nikola said with a weary sigh, as if she were used to this sort of thing. "Go be social, my dearest butterfly."

Ursil cheered happily, leaving Nikola to unload the rest of the fish and start preparing them. He took Lillie's arm and guided her over to the booth three slots down. The woman, barely older than twenty, with long, black braids and a warm smile that lit up as they approached, put her book down.

"Good morning, Ursil. You're up early," she said with a cheeky grin.

"Got someone I want you to meet, Kristin," he

said, nodding to Lillie. "This is Lillie Dean. She moved into that bakery downstairs from Nik and me. Lillie, this is Kristin Honeygold."

"Oh, right!" Kristin's eyes lit up in recognition. "I met your…grandmother? She's…"

"Etheldra, and she's not my grandmother. Just a dear friend," Lillie said. "I do hope she was kind—"

"Kind enough." Kristin cleared her throat. "In any case, she did tell me that you'd be by. Have you used up everything already? You must be baking up a storm."

"Yes, actually," Lillie said. "I also wanted to make your acquaintance. I'm glad you're so close, too. Thought I'd have to go all the way up the hill and out to the farmlands to find what I needed."

"Nah." She beamed. "Goodness, it's so nice to have a real baker on our side of town."

"You don't sell to Mr. Globe?" Lillie asked.

"Bah! He's got his own cows and chickens," she scoffed. "No, us lowly types have to sell to everyone else. But I make a tidy business. My sister and her wife run the farm, and I bring the stuff into town. It's a long way, but it's better than breaking my back milking cows or running after those demonic chickens."

Lillie could relate. "Well, it's lovely to meet you. I'm sure we'll become fast friends."

"Oh! Let me get that box," Ursil said, scampering back to his booth and grabbing one of the pastry boxes. "Here, Kristin. On the house."

"Oh, I don't..." Lillie began but then decided to keep her mouth shut. Best not to offend the closest seller of ingredients she needed. "Try one of the strawberry ones."

Kristin plucked up one of the cupcakes and took a hearty bite. "Oh, my. This is delicious!"

"Oy! Ursil! You up early." Another man came marching up. "Nikola told us to find you to get sommin sweet—is this it?"

"Yeah, help yourself, Dimas," Ursil said.

Lillie winced as the man took a scone then another fisherfolk appeared, who Ursil introduced as Dimas Fryer and their husband Shan. Like the Kovens, they were a married couple with Dimas doing the fishing and Shan doing the mongering. They each took a strawberry cupcake, which they also confessed was the tastiest thing they'd ever eaten in their lives (surprising, considering Lillie had made them two days before).

"I don't—" Lillie began but stopped herself as Ursil waved over two more, twins named Glen and Paul, who took another set, and before Lillie knew it, she was completely out of pastries—and hadn't made a single coin.

"You weren't lying," Glen said, polishing off one of the cupcakes. "How did you make it taste so good, there, girlie?"

"Lillie," she said.

"Hey." Kristin rose with a frown to gesture at the gaggle of fisherfolk. "You lot better pay for those. Lillie started her business, and she ain't giving things out for free. It's hard enough moving to a new town without you eating all her food."

The four fisherfolk shared a look of guilt, and each took a silver out of their pocket and handed it to Lillie before dispersing.

Kristin winked at Lillie then glowered at Ursil. "Nice of you, Ursil. Stealing good food from Lillie."

"It's *advertising*," Ursil said, flapping his hands toward Lillie. "Give 'em a free taste, they'll come back for more."

"Not in this economy," Kristin snapped. "Now you get back to that wife of yours and help her. Goodness knows she's probably exhausted from catching all the fish."

Ursil grumbled but slunk away.

"Well, you certainly have command over the people here," Lillie said with a grin. "And…well, thank you for that. Other than Ursil's gold last night, I haven't made any money the past few days."

"I see why, if you're going to let these oafs take your sweets without paying for them," Kristin said.

"I wasn't planning on…" Lillie began then sighed. "It's a tricky balance, trying to start a new business."

"I can understand that. And if I'm too rough, tell me. My sister-in-law tells me I'm way too blunt for my own good. Probably why I stick to books and not people." She smiled. "But you know, I owe you a silver, too, don't I?"

Lillie hadn't intended to mention it. "We could barter for some eggs and milk?"

"Look, your bakery's off the main street, right? Downstairs from the Kovens?" Lillie nodded. "That's right on my route here. How about I save you a trip tomorrow and drop off some milk and eggs on my way to the market?"

"That would be lovely," Lillie said. "I'm up at four, if you are."

She made a face. "That's too early for my blood. The servants and whatnot like to come get their fresh milk and eggs for their rich folk around seven, so I pass through about six."

"Perfect." Lillie looked around. She didn't see anyone selling flour. "Where do you think I could find a miller? And maybe a chocolate merchant?"

"The rich folks up north get whatever they can't get at the market from Garwood Calcut," Kristin said. "Miriam Handgood can get in touch with him. She works for the elder Mr. Globe himself, so she knows everybody. When I see her, I'll tell her to pass along the message you're looking to buy from him, too." She stopped, looking down the market path, where a gaggle of merchants were walking over. "And you'll probably need him soon. Seems like word's gotten out that there's a pobyd with some delicious baked goods at Ursil's booth."

Lillie walked home with a pocket full of silvers —and a spring in her step. Ursil would get *whatever* he wanted after he'd introduced her to all his friends, and those friends had spread the word, and so on and so forth. When she'd sold her last cupcake, those who'd missed out wanted to know where they could get more, and she was more than happy to tell them to visit the bakery. It seemed Lillie's luck had *finally* changed, and she was looking forward to dreaming up what she was going to bake tomorrow.

"Only thing I need now is to find the local miller," she muttered to herself as she strolled up to the bakery. But as she approached, she stopped short.

There was a letter on the front step. She bent to pick it up. It was addressed to her, but the handwriting wasn't familiar. Nor was there any sign of where it had come from—certainly not Pigsend, and it didn't look like it had come through the post (not that the post was running with any regularity since the queen had been dethroned). She unlocked the front door and stepped inside, opening the letter with her mind on sugar and flour and butter.

But as she scanned the short letter, her heart dropped into her stomach.

Leave Silverkeep, or your new friends find out about what you did in Lower Pigsend

Chapter Five

Lillie stared at the letter, her mouth hanging open. She glanced around, wondering when the blackmailer had dropped the letter off, and if they were watching her.

Well, she wouldn't give them the satisfaction of a response.

She stuffed the letter into her pocket and went back into the bakery. Benetta was the only other person in Silverkeep who knew about her past—perhaps the only person *outside* Lower Pigsend who did, too, other than Bev, and the innkeeper hadn't ever breathed a word about it to anyone. It had been too dangerous to even talk about the existence of the underground haven with Her Majesty's soldiers frequently coming to town.

But why would Benetta send a letter like this when she clearly had no problem being nasty to Lillie's face? Or had someone *else* from Lower Pigsend come to Silverkeep?

Perhaps as mysterious as *who* had sent it was why. Lillie wasn't harming anyone down here, despite what Julian Globe might think. She'd only today made her first sales, and while she had some gold left over from her initial investments, it wasn't as if she was flush with it.

But was that the point? Had someone been watching her all this time, hoping her bakery would fail, and then, when it didn't, sent her a letter to scare her into leaving? And if so…why?

Lillie headed to the window to watch a pair of passersby who, based on their livery, were the servants Ursil had mentioned. If they all worked for the northern-dwellers, then it made sense why they hadn't come into the bakery. Loyalty and all that. Perhaps one of them had sent it, hoping to gain favor with the Globes.

She brought the letter into the kitchen, putting it down next to the cooling loaf of rosemary bread. She tapped the top, thinking fondly of Bev and wishing she were nearby to help her sort through this mess. Bev somehow always came to the answer and made it look easy. Lillie, of course, had been responsible for one of the messes Bev had endured (a fact she felt quite guilty about), but being on the other side left her feeling uneasy.

"What would Bev do?" Lillie said, putting her hands on her hips. "I suppose she'd first try to figure out who knew I came from Lower Pigsend."

That list was short—Benetta.

"The second thing is who would want me to leave town."

That list was also short—Julian. But if that was the case, why send her a letter? Why not threaten her to her face?

Perhaps because he won't travel south of the town square, as Ursil said.

She stared at the letter, sitting next to the loaf of bread made from Bev's recipe. Bev had often complained that she'd been unfairly roped into solving these sorts of problems, because the Pigsend sheriff had been something of a nitwit. Here in Silverkeep, there was a much more intelligent sheriff who seemed keen on resolving issues that came up for the local citizens.

That would, of course, mean Lillie might have to come clean about her past, but as she hadn't done anything *illegal*, perhaps the sheriff would keep mum about the whole thing.

A little after noon, Lillie locked up the bakery

and headed up to the town hall to speak with the sheriff. She rehearsed what to say, especially as she would've preferred *not* to divulge what she'd done in Lower Pigsend. But when she arrived at the town hall, it was filled with an angry crowd shouting down Mr. Abora, who looked even more harried and scattered than usual. Based on the finery of their clothes and the extravagance of their headpieces, Lillie had to assume the crowd were the "northern-dwellers" that Ursil had warned her about—and based on the magical folks sitting on the other side of the hall, Lillie guessed more had come out of hiding to find their property in use.

"That is absolutely unconscionable! There's *no* way I'm moving *my* shop!"

Lillie's attention turned to the front, where Benetta stood, red-faced and barking at Mr. Abora.

"Now, Mrs. Pearlson, calm down," Mr. Abora said, his voice shaky. "There's room for everyone, but some of us will have to make adjustments—"

"Then *she* can make adjustments!" Benetta bellowed. "My family owned that shop and that apartment for *centuries*! I was gone for *six* years—"

"And the queen's rules stated that all magical people forfeited their property when they were arrested," another woman, who Lillie recognized as the seamstress with a shop on the square (presumably Benetta's) said. "I've grown the business from nothing to where it is today. I can't help that you had the misfortune of running afoul of Her Majesty's soldiers."

"I was *never* arrested," Benetta snapped at her. "Check the records."

"None of us were." A man with green skin and pointed ears flapped his arms, which looked more like wings. "And besides that, the queen is gone, and so are her laws."

"How can we be sure she's actually gone, and it's not some big rumor?" the seamstress asked Mr. Abora.

Poor Mr. Abora was struggling to keep the crowd under control. "I understand that there's some confusion. We haven't yet gotten our guidance from…well, whoever's going to be making those decisions. So we're doing the best we can."

"She's dead," Benetta said, waving Mr. Abora off. "And her rules no longer apply."

"Yes, but—"

"It's really quite simple," the green-skinned man said. "Everything should go back to the way it was before. If you had a shop in the town square, you keep your shop in the town square. Otherwise—"

"That means we'll have to move *everyone*," Mr. Abora said.

"Everyone, calm *down*."

An older man who bore a striking resemblance to Julian (without the petulant scowl) rose and strode to the front of the room. His voice was smooth and calming, so much so that Lillie wondered if he didn't have a little magic in him. If Ursil was to be believed, Mr. Globe probably could've paid even Her Majesty's most loyal soldiers to look the other way.

"Now, I know we're all understandably upset and confused," he continued, sitting on the edge of the table. Although he had flecks of gray in his hair, he still exuded youth and vigor, and his dark skin was smooth and without a single wrinkle. "But it doesn't benefit any of us to give our beloved assistant mayor a heart attack."

"T-Thank you, Mr. Globe," Mr. Abora said, his nerves an odd contrast to the calm merchant. "I appreciate the—"

"You have to understand what the world was like six years ago," Mr. Globe continued, his words capturing everyone in the room. "The town had been decimated. We didn't know who was alive and who was in hiding. No idea who might be coming back. So we did the best we could." He gestured to the seamstress. "Maire, here, picked up from a town halfway across the country and moved to Silverkeep so we'd have mended clothes. Jessup over there came to town to ensure our dockworkers had work boots. The rest of the new people have made Silverkeep what it is today—a once-again thriving port on the Pernath Ocean."

He looked around the room, waiting for

someone to argue with him.

"I'm *sure* we can all come to an agreement that suits everyone, one that's fair to the folks who've returned." He nodded to Benetta, who huffed angrily. "And those who've contributed to the growth and success of Silverkeep while they were away."

"The agreement should be that the property comes back to me," Benetta said. "And Maire Gaides can go mend clothes down by the wharf."

"And lose my entire customer base?" Maire huffed. "I don't think so."

Mr. Globe smiled, and for the first time, there was a bit of malice. "As *I'm* the owner of the properties in question, the decision on who the tenant will be actually resides with me."

Lillie looked around the room as everyone shifted uncomfortably. She waited for Benetta to argue more, or even for one of the other folks to stand, but no one did.

"R-right, well," Mr. Abora said, after a too-long pause, "I want everyone to know I've reached out to the powers that be for guidance on how to proceed. There *is* room for everyone, maybe not where you'd prefer. But there's a population down by the docks that needs tailors and cobblers and the like, so it's not as if no one would patronize your business if it moved down there."

Someone muttered, "Yeah, right."

"Rest assured, I'm working on it. It's my top priority—"

"Right after you quit inviting more people to move to town?" Maire asked. "There's a new baker in the south, I saw. Pobyd. Where'd she come from? And why now?"

Lillie's gaze shot to Benetta, waiting for her to spill the beans, but the other seamstress kept quiet.

"Ms. Dean was…something of a late arrival," Mr. Abora said, sounding as if Lillie's appearance had surprised him. "But she's been put down by the wharf. She should be the last of the invitees to arrive."

"Why was she even allowed to come so late?" someone else asked.

Mr. Abora glanced nervously at the elder man beside him, but Mr. Globe said nothing. "Because the wharf needed a bakery," the assistant mayor said, after a moment. "In any case, I think we can all agree that the best way forward is for folks to meet with Mr. Globe—"

"I actually think the *best* way forward is for them to meet with you, so you can come up with a plan for how to proceed," Mr. Globe said to Mr. Abora. "I'm quite busy, Kemp."

"Of course you are, but—"

"Once we have the plan in place, I'll be sure to check in."

With that, Mr. Globe strode out of the town

hall.

Once he was gone, the crowd broke into angry conversations with each other, and no one looked happy, least of all Mr. Abora. Lillie certainly felt for him—he was supposed to be the assistant mayor, not *Mr. Globe's* assistant. But he dutifully took everyone's name down and promised he'd meet with everyone.

"Yes, please provide your name, your current residence—or where you...were, I suppose for the new people," Mr. Abora said. "And the property you claim to own. Then we'll sort it out from there."

Lillie, who'd been about to leave, paused. *Where you were?* If she could check that list, she might be able to find out who else had come from Lower Pigsend. She pulled the threatening letter from her pocket, examining the writing. But when she looked up, she realized with a frown Mr. Abora was writing all the names down. No chance to compare that handwriting, then.

Benetta finished giving her information then turned and met Lillie's gaze with a glare. Lillie stuffed the letter back in her pocket, still unsure what role the Lower Pigsend seamstress had in all this—especially when Benetta smirked and stormed out of the town hall.

Lillie lingered until the angry crowd had dwindled. The folks who currently lived in the town square were *most* eager to remain there, seeming to fear what would happen if they moved to Lillie's part of town. The ones who'd returned from hiding wanted their property back and also didn't want to move down south. Lillie didn't blame either; she'd certainly struggled to get customers her first few days.

"I promise, we will figure this out," Mr. Abora said to the last pair of folks. "Just may take some time. I'll see you tomorrow."

The couple turned to leave, and Mr. Abora sighed in relief, until, of course, he noticed Lillie. "Ah, Ms. Dean. What…can I do for you?"

"I was actually looking for Sheriff Juno," Lillie said, finally looking over to her office, which was closed. "Ah. I see I missed her."

"She's gone off to King's Capital to inquire about how we're supposed to handle all this…" He gestured to the now-empty room. "Silverkeep can't be the only town struggling to navigate these thorny issues. *Someone's* got to have an answer."

"It seems Mr. Globe's asked you to solve it, hasn't he?" Lillie asked. "Does he really own all the property in town?"

"Yes, with very few exceptions," Mr. Abora said. "I do feel for the magical folks who've returned, but I can't… The people who currently live there have been contributing members of the community for years. It's not fair to ask them to leave. Nor is it fair to the folks who *had* to leave when the queen came through."

"They could move down near me at the wharf," Lillie said. "I don't understand why it's so troubling for them to do that."

"Well…" Mr. Abora seemed to consider his words. "It's not so much the location, but the principle of the thing. Why should the current tenants have to move? And why should the previous owners not get their property back?" He sighed. "I haven't the foggiest idea how we're going to fix this."

Lillie tried to catch a glimpse of the sheet. "Has the bakery's previous owner come back?"

"I confess, I don't know off the top of my head." He inspected the paper for a moment. "Doesn't seem like it. But if someone comes to your door, claiming they own it, send them here."

Lillie chewed her lip. "Is there…anyone from Lower Pigsend on the list?"

He stared at her. "Why do you ask?"

"It's the haven I was… I stayed in before…" She cleared her throat, not wanting to get into it. "I saw Benetta Pearlson, she was down there with me. Just curious if anyone else had been hiding there." She nodded to the paper.

"Oh, right. Erm." He scanned the list again. "No, Ms. Pearlson seems to be the only one from Lower…Pigsend."

Lillie didn't love that answer. "I see."

He eyed her. "Why did you want to see Sheriff Juno again?"

"Ah, to see if I could tempt her with a baked good," Lillie said, after a moment's thought. Probably even more important to keep her secret to herself, especially with all the animosity she'd just witnessed. "I don't think she got one the other day, did she?"

"No, but she's not one for sweets," Mr. Abora said, visibly relaxing.

"Ah, well. Back to the shop I go," Lillie said. "It's been...rather quiet the first few days. Luckily, my neighbor Mr. Koven brought me down to the wharf. Lots of interested potential customers there, thankfully." She paused. "I understand there's some...worry about moving to the wharf. But the people are lovely—and clearly, they need the services. It really isn't the worst thing in the world to move down there."

"I quite agree," he said with a smile that didn't reach his eyes. "And I'm glad to hear you've found some customers. They, erm...don't seem bothered by your...?"

"Magic?" Lillie prompted. "No, they don't."

"Wonderful."

"And...when Sheriff Juno comes back, will you send her down to the bakery? I've got a loaf of rosemary bread that I could tempt her with, I'm sure."

"Is that the same recipe as was served at the Weary Dragon?" Mr. Abora asked. "If so, I'd love to come by and get a slice myself."

"It's not quite as good as what Bev makes," she said with a chuckle. "But yes, come by whenever you like."

Chapter Six

Lillie returned to the bakery, letter still stashed in her apron pocket, and considered what to do. With Sheriff Juno gone for who-knew-how-long, Lillie clearly needed to take matters into her own hands. Talking with Benetta seemed the obvious next step. Not that there was a lot of evidence Benetta had written the letter (after all, it was clear the seamstress had more pressing matters to deal with), but perhaps the other woman had mentioned Lillie's past to someone in town, and *that* person was the writer. But getting the seamstress even to talk with Lillie seemed a bridge too far, let alone confess who she might've told about Lillie's past.

"What would Bev do?" she muttered, once again.

Well, once, Bev had asked Lillie to infuse some sugar with truth-telling abilities that she'd baked into a delicious lemon-blueberry bread. Would the same thing work twice?

Lillie spotted the jars of fruit jam she'd brought from Pigsend. They certainly didn't have anything special about them, but if she were to make a new jam, she could infuse the fruit *and* the sugar. Perhaps a thumbprint cookie with a dollop of the jam in the center would do the trick. A small morsel to loosen tongues.

But how to get said morsel onto tongues? There was no way Benetta would willingly eat something Lillie gave her, especially as she knew Lillie's past. But perhaps someone else could serve them—maybe Lillie could have someone deliver them to her?

Before she could get too much farther into her scheming, she ran into her first roadblock—she was out of milk and had no raspberries for the jam. The sun was still out, so presumably, the wharf market was still open, and hopefully, Lillie's new friend Kristin would be there.

It was a short walk, and luckily, Kristin was right where she'd been earlier in the day. The dairy farmer was talking with a man in a dark cloak that nearly swallowed his frame. His pale skin was barely visible through the curtain of black hair that hung around his face, and when he smiled, he was missing a few teeth.

"Oh, Lillie, perfect timing," Kristin said, gesturing to the shadowy man as if he weren't somewhat terrifying. "This is Garwood Calcut. He can get you whatever you need."

"You must be the baker everyone's talking about," he said, his voice wispy and quiet. "It's nice to meet you. I assume you're in need of flour?"

"Y-yes," Lillie said, the merchant unsettling her. "I was hoping to find the closest miller—"

"They're ages away. Better to get your goods from me," he whispered. "How much flour do you need?"

Lillie considered him for a moment. She had already gotten a large bag, and without too many customers, she was being judicious with it. "I'm good on flour for the moment, I think."

"What about cinnamon? Nutmeg?"

All things she already had plenty of. "I think—"

"Chocolate?"

"Oh yes, please," Lillie said. "Chocolate bars and cocoa powder would be excellent."

"I've already got a shipment of chocolate coming for the Globe Café this evening," he said softly. "Maybe I can cleave off a bit for you."

"Oh, don't do that," Lillie said with a wave of her hand. "He already hates me enough."

Mr. Calcut gave her a sideways look. "A bit of advice for you, since I hear you're new to business: don't look a gift horse in the mouth. Mr. Globe won't miss a few pounds of chocolate—from what I hear, he throws out most of it. So take the chocolate from me."

Lillie glanced at Kristin, hoping for her approval, which she gave emphatically. "Listen to him, he's the best merchant in the harbor."

"Don't say that too loudly," he said. "I've got enemies, you know. Don't want to make any more." He tapped his nose. "I'll drop the chocolate off later today."

"Thank you," Lillie said, as he slipped down the street. "Is he…"

"Creepy? Absolutely," Kristin said with a laugh. "But he's the best. I don't know where he gets half of what he gets. If you need *anything*, no matter how weird, he can find it for you."

"Interesting…" Lillie eyed the way he'd gone.

"You certainly were walking with purpose," Kristin said. "Busy day at the bakery?"

"I was about to make some, erm…" Lillie thought for a moment. "Cookies. But I remembered I was all out of eggs and milk for butter."

"Hard to make cookies without that," Kristin said. "They wouldn't be…chocolate chip cookies, would they?"

"No, I was thinking raspberry thumbprint,"

Lillie said.

"Not as good as chocolate chip, but I'd eat one anyway," Kristin said.

"Oh, they're not..." She might need to make *two* batches of cookies. "Erm, well, someone's ordered them, so—"

"Look at you, making money." Kristin grinned. "How much milk do you need?"

Lillie bought one jug of milk and a dozen eggs, and, after paying, she asked Kristin to point her in the direction of the best farmer to buy produce from. The dairy farmer took it upon herself to introduce Lillie to Ewing Dupont, a sweet old man with wrinkles that sagged into his eyes and a smile that seemed too big for his face. He had a large cone that he used to hear, and when he spoke, his volume was louder than it should've been. But he had a pound of raspberries and was happy to sell them to Lillie.

"That should set me up for this afternoon, in any case," Lillie said, juggling the carton of raspberries and eggs in one arm, and the jug in the other.

"You should bring a basket next time," Kristin said.

"Right, probably should," Lillie replied. "Had a bit of a one-track mind today. Just so...excited someone ordered a dozen cookies. Selling one or two per person is nice, of course, but getting a large order for a birthday cake or something like that is always nice."

"Oh, you make birthday cakes?" Kristin said, scratching her chin. "Good to know. I tried to order one from that café on the north side of town for my sister's birthday a few weeks ago. Was told they don't do that kind of thing. Can you believe that? A bakery that doesn't make cakes."

Lillie demurred instead of voicing her real opinion. "Well, I'm happy to make whatever you like. You've been such a dear friend to me already, and we've only known each other a few hours."

"Yes, but I have a feeling you're about to double my business," she said with a wink. "We took a hit during the war, financially—big one. My parents used to raise tanddaes—you know what those are?"

Lillie nodded. "Magical sheep with purple wool."

"Yeah, well, they're *highly* illegal. So of course, when that queen came to power, and her soldiers tore through here, they arrested my folks for having 'em. No idea where they are now."

"Oh, Kristin, I'm so sorry," Lillie said. "That's awful. And you don't know where—?"

"I got an idea, but it's not polite to say," she said darkly. "In any case, I don't think I'll ever believe we're really safe from those goons. You're real brave for coming out with your pobyd-ness. If I had magic, I certainly wouldn't be advertising it." Then, as if a switch had flipped in her mind, Kristin brightened again. "You'd better be getting back to bake before you drop all that stuff."

Lillie shook herself at the abrupt change in conversation. "Will you be by in the morning?"

She nodded. "And you'd better have a dozen chocolate chip cookies waiting for me!"

"If Mr. Calcut comes through, they'll be ready for you," Lillie replied.

Back home, Lillie made a beeline for the kitchen, where she put down all the goods she'd purchased. She started a fire in her oven then poured the milk into a bowl and coaxed it to stir itself into a frenzy. One of the *many* perks of being a pobyd was that she could convince ingredients to mix themselves—or in this case, milk to spin and spin until the butter solids separated from the liquid.

While that worked, Lillie portioned the sugar she'd need for the jam and cookies into a separate bowl. Then she bent down to stare into the mound of white crystals, narrowing her gaze until it was all she could see. She thought about every time she'd ever felt compelled to tell the truth, when she *needed* someone to know what was on her heart, until the feeling filled her from tip to toe. Magic hummed in her blood, swirling around in her mind and making her a little dizzy.

"Now listen here," she said to the bowl. "I know

sugar has all kinds of secrets that you're dying to spill. You want to reveal everything about where you've been and what you've done, and what kind of letters you might have written recently. Tell me everything on your mind and in your heart, and don't stop until every secret has been revealed."

The sugar, predictably, didn't respond, but her throat itched to tell more secrets, so she grabbed the two cases of raspberries and placed them in front of her.

"You, too, raspberries. So many secrets. I'm sure you've seen a lot while growing on your vines. And those who picked you have much to share. So share what's on your red little hearts, and tell me everything I want to know."

She stood up, her head swimming with magic and her tongue on fire. She took a few deep breaths to steady herself, wondering if perhaps she'd overdone it or if she was feeling the effects because she was in such a small space. She walked out of the kitchen into the shopfront and stared out the window. The day was wearing on, and Lillie grew increasingly agitated at the number of people who walked by her store without coming in.

"One day, I'll convince them all that I'm worth taking a chance on," Lillie muttered then realized she'd spoken aloud. One of the *unintended* consequences of infusing magic was that she, too, became influenced by it. The feeling would fade, eventually, but right now, the urge to confess everything she'd ever done wrong and all her hopes, fears, and dreams about Silverkeep was almost overwhelming.

"Not that anyone's keen to hear that," she said, picking up her broom and sweeping the clean floor.

Keeping herself busy, and distracting her mind, was essential to not getting carried away by it. Perhaps with practice, she might be able to infuse magic without this annoying aftereffect.

"But should I actually be practicing this?" she said, grabbing a rag and cleaning every surface she could find. "Maybe I can sell it. Lillie's truthful confections. Find out if your partner is cheating on you, or if your neighbor's lying about where they dump their refuse." She snorted then considered it. "Not a bad idea, actually."

Still, she couldn't shake the jitters. She didn't dare go into the kitchen yet, not until the feeling had fully passed. She didn't want to risk being reinfluenced. Not when every secret she'd ever kept was threatening to come to the surface.

"Dangerous game you're playing, Lillie. What if someone came in and wanted to talk with you? You'd spill your guts then and there." She shook her head. "Steady on, girl. Deep breaths. This feeling will pass."

The longer it lingered, the more she thought this *wasn't* something she wanted to sell. She couldn't spend her life feeling like she was going to blurt out the first thing that came to mind. And it wasn't as if she could step outside for a walk, either. Too many people around.

Her tongue itched so much that she chewed on it, then, after a moment, sighed heavily. "Fine. Here's my confession. Things were good in Pigsend, even if I was working for Allen—who I like, by the way. I just didn't love having to *answer* to him. And I wanted to be alone in *my* bakery, as silly as it sounds. And Pigsend was lovely, but after what I did in Lower Pigsend, I wanted a fresh start. How wonderful to be *invited* to go somewhere. That my skills were so good they impressed Mr. Abora. But now…"

She sighed, looking at the rag in her hand.

"Now, I wonder if I was too rash in leaving. The gold I have won't last forever. And one or two customers aren't cutting it. I don't have a steady stream of business, either. Not with the inn, and not with Mr. Globe, though he could *obviously* use my help." She scowled. "And what's the big idea with him, being mean for no reason? It's not *my* fault he can't bake his way out of a paper bag. Clearly, no one cares." She stopped, snorting. "Maybe I should start baking horrible things, too. It's clear that's what the people of Silverkeep want."

She stopped, closing her eyes. None of this truth-telling was making her feel any better. Perhaps because it was all a mask for what she was really feeling.

"I'm scared," she whispered, "that I've made the wrong decision about moving to Silverkeep."

"That's too bad."

Lillie jumped, the rag flying from her hand as she spun toward the source of the voice. Mr. Calcut stood in the doorway to the kitchen. She shivered, wondering how someone could be in broad daylight but still appear drenched in shadow—and how much of her *confession* he'd heard.

"W-what? I'm sorry, did you say something?" Lillie said, after a moment. Her tongue still threatened to unleash all her hopes, fears, and everything in-between to the merchant, but she inhaled deeply and smoothed her apron.

"I'm here with the chocolate you requested," he said, brandishing a bag from out of nowhere. "Payment is one gold coin."

Lillie eyed the bag, finding it a bit small for the price. But she *was* in somewhat desperate need of it. "May I see it? I'm not sure..." She swallowed her thought. *Watch it.* "I want to check it first."

"By all means."

He glided over, handing her the bag. It was weightier than Lillie would've guessed, and inside, she found five neat bars of chocolate. It would be enough to get her going for sure and make a double batch of the chocolate chip cookies Kristin had been after.

"Is it up to your standards?" he asked, flashing her a smile.

"Yes, this will do nicely." She crossed the kitchen to where she kept her stash of gold coins. There weren't quite as many left as she'd hoped, but she could justify this expense—especially for good quality chocolate. "Here you go. Is…this the price going forward? One gold coin for five bars of chocolate?"

"Is that the price you're willing to pay?" he asked.

Lillie considered him. Perhaps it was the truth magic still loosening her tongue, but she felt brave. "Today, yes. Tomorrow, who knows? It's a little higher than I'd prefer, but I understand that this was a special case." She eyed him. "How about one gold for ten bars?"

He whistled, which perhaps came through one of his missing teeth. "That's quite a lot of chocolate. It's not like it's *easy* to obtain. And I'm the only one in town who can."

"Are you?" Lillie eyed him. "Maybe I'll ask Kristin—"

"Eight bars for a gold coin," he said. "Plus, a sweet of my choice when I bring by the goods."

"Eight bars, plus a pound of cocoa powder, and you can take two sweets of your choice," Lillie countered.

He considered that for a long while, then cracked a smile. "You drive a hard bargain, Ms. Dean. But I think we've got a deal."

"Excellent." Lillie smiled and gestured to the front case. "Please, help yourself to whatever you like today."

He nodded his head, then, after raiding the display case for a cookie and muffin, was gone.

Lillie shivered, sensing there was something amiss about him, but grateful she had one of the key ingredients no baker should be without. And eight chocolate bars for a gold coin was actually a *better* deal than Allen had with his merchant. She was somewhat pleased with herself that she'd managed to go toe to toe with Mr. Calcut and come out victorious. Perhaps the *only* thing that had gone right since she'd moved here...

Chapter Seven

Lillie assembled the cookies, combining the butter and sugar, then adding an egg, flour, and salt, until the dough came together. As she spooned individual portions, magic zinged her fingertips, and her tongue itched once more. She glanced at the raspberries, macerating with the magic-infused sugar, and winced.

"Maybe I overdid it."

She was able to convince the sugar to give up *some* magic, and hoped the heat from the oven might release more of it. She didn't want Benetta to spill every secret she had, after all. Lillie only wanted to know who'd written the letter, or who else in town knew about Lower Pigsend.

Lillie had to step outside as the cookies baked to get some fresh air and clear her mind. But every time she went back inside, truths threatened to spill out of her like a waterfall and her half-baked plan seemed to make *more* sense. After all, she wanted the truth, so why not go get it? The only problem, really, was how to trick Benetta into eating a cookie.

She was having visions of opening Benetta's mouth and cramming a thumbprint cookie down her throat when the bell over the front door tinkled. Lillie frowned, looking through the opening. Had Mr. Calcut had come back? Instead three fisherfolk were inspecting the contents of her display case.

She gasped. "My first in-store customers!"

Quickly, she wiped her hands, plastering on a too-bright smile and taking a few deep breaths to steady herself and get a hold of the magic still swimming in her mind. She hoped the other three wouldn't be quite so affected by it, but perhaps a spot of magic might entice them to buy more pastries.

"Hello there," Lillie said, her voice a little *too* loud. "Welcome to the Pobyd Perfections Bakery. So glad to have you here."

"Ursil Koven told us we needed to come down and get a sweet," one of the men, who smelled strongly of fish and wore a pair of waders that looked like he'd come straight out of the water. "Name's Abraham Roudie."

"Oh, wonderful to meet you," Lillie said, scurrying around to the bakery case. She turned to the other two, recognizing them as the twins Glen and Paul Jacob who'd snatched a few sweets earlier in the day. They smiled bashfully at her as she beamed at them. "And lovely to see you two again, as well. I hope this means you'll be regular customers. What can I tempt you with this afternoon?"

Mr. Roudie opted for one of the muffins, and the twins purchased a scone and cupcake each. They sat at the tables with their wares, but the shop was so small that they were still in conversation distance. The twins went to town wordlessly, having already sampled Lillie's confections, but Mr. Roudie let out a gasp of surprise when he bit into the muffin.

"What in the world did you put in this?" he said. "It's amazing!"

"Love" was usually Lillie's response, back when the queen's people lurked around every corner. But today, she was feeling brave—and also perhaps a little addled with magic. "Pobyds can infuse ingredients with intentions. I told that flour it had better be the most delicious thing in the world when I made those muffins."

"Well, it surely listened," Mr. Roudie said. "You boys might have to get behind me for tomorrow's opening hours. When *do* you open?"

"I'm in the bakery around four, but we open at seven," Lillie said, pleased she could perhaps count on three customers tomorrow. "I know Mr. Ursil's looking forward to getting some muffins. Any requests?"

"Just keep making 'em this good," Mr. Roudie said. He brought his empty plate to her. "Leave this with you?"

"Happy to take it." She beamed at him. "You know, you three are my first real customers. So you've got a special place in my heart."

"Does that mean we get a discount?" Glen asked, and his brother shushed him loudly.

"Maybe when I've got more than three customers a day," Lillie replied, then realized she was once again speaking too frankly but unable to stop herself. "I was hoping to get a partnership with the Silverkeep Inn, but Ms. Lyle doesn't want to partner with me."

"She doesn't like to partner with anyone," Mr. Roudie said. "Not since that Mr. Globe gave her an indoor job. Suddenly, she's too good to be seen with us dockworkers. But she's always been a bit too big for her waders. Even when we were kids."

"Oh, you…grew up together?" The salt air and sun had aged Mr. Roudie more than Ms. Lyle, as Lillie would've guessed the innkeeper was twenty years his junior. "That means…I suppose you were here when the purge happened, weren't you?"

He nodded. "Strange times, then. Went from a town full of life to practically empty. Then everyone who got invited here moved into the square, and this part of town never recovered."

"It may yet," Lillie said. "With the queen being defeated—"

"Bah. I heard that rumor. Don't believe it myself," Mr. Roudie said. "Seems too good to be true, you know?"

"Folks are coming back, though," Lillie said, hoping she might get something out of these three she hadn't gotten elsewhere. "Which is causing problems up in the town square."

Paul snorted. "Oh yeah? What kinda problems do those rich folks have?"

"The magical folks who were run off," Lillie said, watching their expressions closely. "The ones who managed to escape Her Majesty, they're coming back. Finding strangers in their property. I was at the town hall earlier today, and Benetta Pearlson was up in arms because someone else owns her seamstress shop."

"Benetta's alive?" Mr. Roudie's entire face brightened, and he looked a few years younger. "And she's back?"

Lillie nodded, sensing a golden opportunity. "You were close?"

"I don't know about close, but..." His cheeks

had gone rosy. "I was certainly quite fond of her back in the day."

"That's a name I haven't heard in a while," Glen said, looking at his brother. "What happened to her? She was out loud with her magic, wasn't she? Did she get taken away by the queen's people?"

"She was in hiding," Lillie said, trying to keep her excitement to a minimum. "But I saw her back in town yesterday. She's keen on getting her seamstress shop back, I believe. Someone else had taken over her location, and she was going to speak with Mr. Globe about it." She paused. "The older one."

"Yeah, we know who you meant. Usually only one person comes to mind when you say 'Mr. Globe,'" Roudie said.

"What do you…know about her?" Lillie asked. "Benetta."

"Well, at the time the queen came through town," Roudie said, "there really wasn't much of a difference between rich or poor. If you had magic, you were gone the next morning. Don't surprise me Benetta Pearlson could've skipped town instead of being taken away like so many others. Probably paid a pretty penny to a soldier or two—she had all kinds of money before the war."

The seamstress certainly didn't look like she had much now, with her threadbare clothes and worn shoes.

"I'll have to find her and pay her a visit," Roudie said. "Maybe she'll want to give me the time of day now that she's poor like the rest of us."

"She didn't before?" Lillie asked, unable to believe her luck. Benetta probably wouldn't take a cookie from Lillie, but she might take one from an old friend.

"Well, I think she was keener on men of the merchant class. A dock repairman such as myself makes a decent living, but who wants to come home to a partner smelling of fish and the sea?" He chuckled, and Lillie realized that this sweet old man had harbored a crush on awful Benetta all these years. From what Lillie knew of her, she didn't deserve his affection.

"I think any person would like that," Lillie said. "The Kovens seem to have a happy marriage."

"Yeah, but that's because they *both* come home smelling like the sea," he said. "But maybe if Benetta doesn't have her spot to the north, she might be convinced to move in across the street."

Benetta had acted like moving to this side of town was worse than death, so Lillie doubted the seamstress would come willingly.

"You know," Lillie started slowly, "I've got a batch of raspberry thumbprint cookies I was going to take to Benetta myself. They're cooling now, and I'm about to add the jam to them. Would you like to take them to her instead? Might help sweeten the greeting if you come with cookies, you know?"

His eyes lit up, and Lillie caught a small glint of affection in them. "Oh, that would be wonderful. I do recall Benetta loving raspberry, too. That's awfully kind of you, Ms. Dean." He reached into his pocket and placed two silvers on the counter. "I insist on paying for them."

"Call me Lillie," she said, feeling guilty for taking the silvers, but she needed the money. "And I'm happy to help. Who doesn't love a second-chance romance?"

And if she could get the truth out of her Lower Pigsend neighbor, all the better.

Mr. Roudie headed home to get washed up and changed, and Lillie set to finishing up the cookies. The truth-telling magic was still quite potent, but the cookies were small enough that maybe it wouldn't cause that much trouble if Benetta only ate one. Lillie was hoping to follow Mr. Roudie and intervene with her questions as soon as the magic took effect. It made sense in her mind, though she had to keep hold of her tongue so she wouldn't tell Mr. Roudie all about her plans.

The dock worker returned an hour later, wearing a nice shirt and clean pants, and his gray hair had been combed and slicked over. He'd also procured a bouquet of flowers and looked quite put-together.

"You look so handsome," Lillie said, instead of

telling him that the cookies were spiked with magic. "Benetta's going to be so surprised to see you."

"Do you know where she's staying?" Mr. Roudie asked.

"The Silverkeep Inn, I believe. That's where all the returned folks are staying," Lillie replied. "I saw at least five in the town hall this afternoon. They're all angry with each other. People who returned wanted their homes back. People who've been here wanted…" She clamped her mouth closed until she could get a hold of herself. "In any case, you're very handsome."

Mr. Roudie didn't seem to notice her struggle. "Six years it's been since I've seen her! Hope she recognizes me. Don't think she had any other boyfriends while she was…where did you say she was?"

"Lower Pigsend," Lillie said.

"Right, that's… Well, I'm sure it was a lovely place." He nodded to the box in her hand. "Are those for me?"

"Yes, of course." Lillie all but thrust them over. "Erm… You know, people are always touched when a potential lover goes the extra mile." She flashed a smile as the lie became increasingly hard to tell. "You…could say…you…baked them."

"Oh, she wouldn't believe me," Mr. Roudie said, with a bashful chuckle.

"I bet she would." Lillie beamed. "Trust me:

you'll want to take all the credit for this."

Mr. Roudie thanked her again then set off for the Silverkeep Inn, not once looking back. Lillie waited a few minutes to give him a head start then followed, ready to enact part two of her plan. First, Benetta would eat a cookie. Then she'd spill her guts, and Lillie would find out...

Lillie slowed. The farther she got from the magic-filled bakery, not to mention the magic-filled cookies, the clearer her mind became—and slowly, horror descended as she realized what she'd done.

She'd sent a sweet old man with *magic-laced* cookies to a woman who *would know* those cookies came from Lillie—and who would *perhaps* be a bit put out by the spellcasting.

Or worse, Benetta would blame Mr. Roudie for the magic-laced cookies, thus preventing him from rekindling with his old flame.

And worst of all, *Mr. Roudie* knew where he got the cookies, and if Benetta started speaking the truth to him, based on their history...

"I have to get those cookies!"

Lillie put on a burst of speed, hoping to catch Mr. Roudie before he met up with Benetta, but when she reached the inn, the duo were in the front room, Mr. Roudie standing with the box tucked under his arm, and Benetta glaring at him with a cup of tea. At least the box was unopened.

"I—oh." Mr. Roudie frowned as he turned.

"What are you doing here?"

"Erm, I apologize," Lillie said, stepping forward quickly. "I tasted the jam right after you left, and I'm horrified to tell you that I think I used salt instead of sugar."

"But I was telling Ms. Pearlson here that I made 'em," he said, giving her a look that very clearly said he wanted Lillie to stop talking.

"Well, trust me when I say, you won't want to eat them," Lillie said with a wide smile she hoped appeared sincere and not petrified.

"A pobyd? Messing up a recipe?" Benetta drawled, raising her eyebrow. "Unheard of."

"Well, I'm not sure where my brain is," Lillie said, inching toward Mr. Roudie. "Maybe I can—"

But Mr. Roudie yanked the box out of her reach. "No, I made 'em. Because I'm so happy to see Benetta again, remember? All that about effort and her believing me?"

"Yes, but they're…" Lillie made a face. "Quite salty."

"I like salt." Benetta held out her hand. "Let me try."

"No!" Lillie jumped forward and slammed her hand down on the box, sending the cookies flying to the ground. Thankfully, they landed jam-side-down on the inn floor.

"What have you done?" Mr. Roudie gasped.

"*Yes*, Lillie, what *have* you done?" Benetta asked.

"Saved you all from a salty fate," Lillie said, quickly canvassing the room and picking up every last cookie. "I'm so terribly sorry, Mr. Roudie. Please forgive me. But I couldn't let you give them to her. She'd…" That *stupid* magic was infiltrating her brain again as a bit of the jam got on her finger. "It wouldn't have been good."

"Well, Roudie, I think it's *clear* a fairy doesn't change its wings," Benetta said, sitting back and smiling at Lillie. "She's *full* of treachery and would backstab you the moment she got a chance. I wouldn't be caught dead patronizing her store. I do hope you didn't *pay* for those."

Roudie looked between the two of them, unsure what to say.

Lillie's cheeks warmed. "I'm happy to give you a refund," she whispered.

"I think it's time you leave," Benetta snapped. "Unless you have something else you wish to poison me with?"

Lillie stared between the two of them, swallowing her words. She should've balled up her confidence and demanded to know from Benetta if she'd written the nasty letter—or, better yet, who else knew about her past in Lower Pigsend. After all, she'd gone to all this trouble, and she might as well get something out of it. But her mouth went dry, especially as Mr. Roudie glared at her. She'd already caused enough damage—perhaps the letter-writer wasn't all that far off and she *should* leave town.

So without anything else to say, Lillie took her box of dirty cookies and left.

Chapter Eight

Lillie felt *awful*.

She carried the thumbprint cookies back to the bakery and promptly tossed them, along with the remaining raspberry jam. She didn't want to risk someone else seeing them and wanting to eat them. Not that *anyone* would be coming to her bakery after Mr. Roudie spread the word. She couldn't get his look of surprise out of her mind, and the way Benetta had so accurately described her as a *backstabber*.

If the apron fit…

As the sun set, Lillie locked up and snuck up to

her apartment, leaning against the door with a sigh. She couldn't shake the feeling that—once again—she'd acted rashly and messed up a perfectly good thing. Benetta was probably telling Mr. Roudie all about Lillie's history in Lower Pigsend, and soon the entire wharf would know how rotten Lillie really was at her core.

Lillie padded over to the tiny kitchenette and pulled out the half-loaf of bread from the night before. She could've cast a freshening spell to liven it back up, but she didn't feel that hungry, especially not for rosemary bread and all the memories it elicited. Lillie's gaze went to the quill, ink, and paper on the small desk, and her guilt grew. Bev would be sorely disappointed.

Not that it mattered anymore. All the goodwill she'd amassed the day before with Ursil would evaporate. She'd run out of money, and she'd have to return to Pigsend with her tail between her legs.

She tossed and turned all night, imagining Benetta leading the charge to her front door, demanding she leave town. She rose late, scowling at her reflection in the mirror, and headed down to the bakery. She didn't even turn on the oven, knowing in her gut that she wouldn't be selling anything today. So she cast a freshening spell on the things in her window. Saving her few remaining gold coins was more important than keeping to the Pobyd Perfections standard.

She was wallowing in a cup of tea, wiping tears from her eyes, when there was a knock at the back door. She glanced at the clock with a frown then hurried to the back, opening the door to reveal Kristin's smiling face.

"Morning," she said. "Brought you a few jugs of milk and some eggs."

"Oh, Kristin." Lillie had completely forgotten about their agreement. "I'm so sorry. I'm not sure…"

"That's all right. It's early in your business. Probably not selling enough to make more. Take 'em anyway. I'm sure you can do something with them." She stepped inside, placed the jugs and dozen eggs on the counter, and looked around expectantly. "Where are my cookies? Don't tell me Mr. Calcut didn't come through with the chocolate. It's not like him to—"

"He did," Lillie said softly. "I'm sorry. I didn't think anyone would be by today."

Kristin narrowed her eyes. "What's wrong? You look like someone stole your favorite kitten."

Lillie sighed. "I…made a mistake yesterday. I was trying to figure out…" She licked her lips. Perhaps a sanitized version of the truth would satisfy Kristin. "Someone sent me a letter that threatened to divulge a secret if I didn't leave town. I thought I knew who'd done it, so I used a bit of magic to try to coax out the truth. But I…made a mess of it."

"You can use magic to make people tell the truth?" Kristin said with a wry grin. "That's pretty useful."

"Not when you take advantage of a nice man's heart," Lillie said. "In any case, it's put me in a… Well, I'm sure I won't get a single customer once word gets out. I'm considering moving back to Pigsend."

"Pshaw. Do you think you're the first person around these parts with a devastating secret?" Kristin said. "We all got 'em. I doubt yours is bad enough that you'd be run out of town on a rail."

"You'd be surprised."

"If Mr. Globe can pay the soldiers to take his butler to the queen's jail in his place and still command the respect of the town, I'd say you're okay."

Lillie's eyes widened. "What?"

"Well, it's not confirmed," Kristin said. "But a lot of us thought Globe had magic or dealt with it. I mean, a man with his wealth, it would've been stranger if he hadn't. But when the queen's goons came to town, his butler was the one carted off—and my sister says that man hadn't shown as much as a spark of magic in his life. Still, who's going to say anything against Audo Globe?"

"Who indeed?" Lillie said. "There's one large difference between the two of us. He's got lots of money. Mine's quickly running out. And I thought, after yesterday, that perhaps I'd turned a corner. But I was so focused on my own cleverness, I forgot to pay attention to the bigger picture."

"Well, make something chocolate so I can pay you a silver for it, then you'll start making more money." She patted Lillie on the shoulder. "Look, I can tell whatever you did is eating at you. Maybe whoever you did it to would accept an apology—especially if you tell him why you did it. I mean, I also kinda want to know who sent you a threatening letter—and what kinda dirt they have on you that you'd consider leaving town." She scrutinized Lillie. "You'd didn't off anyone, did you?"

"Goodness, no," Lillie said with a laugh that quickly dissipated. "But if I'd succeeded, a large number of people would've been in danger. Thankfully, I was stopped, but I can't help thinking about what might've happened if I hadn't been."

"Eh, that doesn't sound so bad," Kristin said. "I think you're making a mountain out of a molehill."

Lillie snorted at the word *mole*. "Clearly, whoever sent me this letter thinks that this secret is worth blackmailing over."

"Or someone's hoping you'll scare easy," Kristin said. "I mean, everyone's acting squirrelly since the rumor started that the queen was gone and magical folk started showing up in town again. I heard Ursil saying the other day that he thought it was a ruse to get all the magical folk left behind to come out of the woodwork, so the queen's people can ride into town and snatch them up."

"That does sound like something she'd do," Lillie said. "But I have it on very good authority that the queen's been defeated."

"Well, good to know." Kristin rose. "I've got to get the rest of the product off the wagon at my booth before the rich folks' servants arrive." She tilted her head at Lillie. "I know you think that you've made a mess of things, but I've never known anyone to make *such* a mess that they couldn't be forgiven. Especially if they're as bent outta shape about it as you are. So I say you bake up some of those cookies, bring me some, and take the rest to whomever you've wronged. The worst they can say is no, and you'll know you've done your part to make things right."

Lillie nodded. "You know, I might do that. Thank you, Kristin." Her smile widened. "And I'll be sure to bring you a batch of cookies as soon as they're ready."

As soon as the loquacious dairy farmer left, Lillie headed right into the kitchen to gather flour, sugar, milk, and the bars of chocolate and get a fire going in her oven. First, she picked up one of the two cream jugs Kristin had brought and poured the milk into a large bowl. She tapped the bowl with her finger to remove the heat from it, leaving it nice and cold, then swirled the liquid with her finger. The swirling continued, faster and faster, until the mixture was whipping itself.

While that worked, she grabbed her sharpest knife and carefully diced the chocolate bars. By now, the butter had separated from the milk, so she scooped it out, rinsed it off under the hand pump outside, then placed it in another bowl.

To that, she added the sugar and a bit of molasses for color then took a wooden spoon and beat the mixture until it was nice and fluffy. In another bowl, she added flour and salt, along with leavening, tipped that into the dough a little at a time, and let her mind wander.

Kristin had made her feel somewhat better about her predicament. If everyone in Silverkeep had their secrets, then perhaps they wouldn't think too poorly of Lillie for hers. Not that she was going to tell everyone, but people knowing might not be as dire as Lillie had initially thought.

Still, it was important to make amends with Mr. Roudie, at least. She could afford to make enemies up north, but the wharf folks were her only customers.

When the mixture was just combined, she dumped the chocolate chunks into the mixture and folded them in gently. She grabbed one of her baking sheets and carefully spooned out a little at a time. The mixture made about four dozen cookies, and she happily tossed the first two sheets into her oven.

"There," Lillie said to herself. "Cookies for the one person in Silverkeep who still wants to be my friend."

The cookies took no time to bake, so Lillie swapped out the baking sheets for the second set then placed the first on a cooling rack. They smelled heavenly, and although she hadn't *intentionally* infused them with magic, a bit always seeped into the dough as she worked it. Just to be absolutely on the safe side, she concentrated on pulling any remaining pobyd magic out of the cookies. They'd be delicious by themselves, just not exquisite. But she wanted to offer Mr. Roudie cookies completely without any traces of magic.

When the second batch (with magic) came out, it was close to nine. Lillie anxiously watched the front window for the next hour, wondering if Ursil would come by or if the rumor mill had already started. As the clock struck ten, she'd all but convinced herself he wouldn't show up, but five minutes after, he strolled in, looking joyful.

"Mornin', you! What's on the menu today?" He inhaled deeply. "I smell chocolate."

"Well, I've just pulled some cookies out of the oven," Lillie said, wiping her hands. "But I've got a selection from yesterday, too."

"Did I hear something about raspberry

thumbprint cookies, too?" He patted his stomach. "I do love raspberry."

"Erm, those are... I can make more," Lillie said quickly. "With jam from Pigsend. I got a late start this morning for...reasons." She shifted. "You haven't seen Mr. Roudie today, have you?"

"Not yet, but I'm sure he's down at the docks." He frowned. "Why? He wasn't rude to you, was he? Not pay his bill?"

"Nothing like that. I actually owe him an apology," Lillie said.

"Last I heard, he was repairin' a dock on the east side of things, over where Nik has her dinghy," he said. "I'd be happy to take you...for a price."

The price was a cookie, which Lillie was happy to pay, and together, they walked down to the market again. Lillie's first stop, of course, was to drop a box of chocolate chip cookies off with Kristin, who was happy to get the goodies but happier to see Lillie had shaken off the dark cloud.

"You're much more pleasant when you aren't down in the dumps," she said, chowing down on the first cookie. "Oh, man. Yeah. You gotta sell these. You won't keep 'em in stock if you do."

"Agreed," Ursil said with a nod, peering into the other box. "You don't think—"

"There'll be more at the bakery later today," Lillie said. "Now where are the southeastern docks?"

Lillie followed Ursil's instructions, walking to

the very end of the market and out onto the wooden planks that stretched into the deep, blue water. Unlike the other side of the wharf, the ships here were one- or two-person vessels, large enough to haul in a catch of fish but not much else. Glen and Paul were talking to two people Lillie hadn't met. The quartet scented the cookies and spun on Lillie as she walked by.

"Whatcha got there, Lillie?" Glen asked, nodding to the box. "Are you making deliveries now?"

"We were gonna stop by on our lunch break," Paul said. "Bringing these two yahoos as well." He nodded to the others. "This is Orxan and Jan McTavish."

"Pleased to meet you," Lillie said, barely acknowledging them as they surveyed her closely. "Is Mr. Roudie around?"

"Ah, more sweets for his ladylove, eh?" Paul said with a knowing look. "He's over there."

He pointed to the end of the dock, and Lillie frowned. "Where?"

"In the water."

She walked to the edge and peered down, surprised to see Mr. Roudie waist-deep in the water, hammer and nails in hand as he worked on repairing a part of the piling that went into the water. He glanced up then jolted in surprise, almost dropping all his tools.

"I'm so sorry. I didn't mean to scare you!" Lillie said, kneeling. "I wanted to apologize for what happened yesterday."

"Oh, yeah, that was a mean trick to play on me," he said, his frown not leaving. "What was wrong with those cookies anyway?"

Lillie figured the best balm was the truth—all of it. Benetta had probably told him the worst about her anyway. "Well, to be honest, I received a threatening letter about my past, saying they'd reveal everything if I didn't leave Silverkeep. I assumed Benetta wrote it, as she's the only person who knew me from Lower Pigsend. So I thought..." She shook her head. "I *didn't* think. I took advantage of your kindness. And for that, I'm so terribly sorry."

He eyed her, bobbing in the water. There was a harness wrapped around the piling to keep him afloat.

"A-anyway, I brought you a new batch of cookies. No magic, I promise. Not even a pobyd amount. I wanted..." She sighed deeply. "I really feel awful, Mr. Roudie. Both about giving Benetta the spelled cookies and lying to you. I swear I won't do it again." She paused. "Benetta told you all about my past, didn't she?"

"She...didn't, actually," Roudie said. "I mean, don't get me wrong, she complained about you being backstabby and treacherous and rude, but that was only for a minute. She spent the rest of the time complainin' about Mr. Abora and Mr. Globe." He cracked a smile. "She let me sit there and listen to her complain for near three hours! It was the best night ever."

Lillie nearly fell off the dock. "Really?"

"And she told me as long as I don't bring anything else you bake to her, I could come back tonight, and she'd complain some more." He finished with a bright smile. "So suppose I should be thankin' you for getting me in the door."

Lillie hardly thought listening to Benetta vent for hours was a romantic evening, but she was thrilled no harm had been done. "I'm so happy to hear that."

"I figure if dislikin' you is what gets me a second date with her," he smiled broadly, "then she can think I don't like you. And I can still come get a scone or a muffin from you, providin' you don't put anythin' weird into them."

"Wouldn't dream of it," Lillie said, picking up the box and showing Mr. Roudie what was inside. "Chocolate chip. Absolutely no magic at all in them —I made sure. But if you'd rather I take them with me…"

"No, no." He reached a wet hand inside and snatched one. "Leave 'em. Nice to have something to munch on while I work. As long as you don't tell Benetta—"

"I won't say a word."

CHAPTER NINE

Lillie returned to the bakery, full of happiness once more. She didn't *quite* understand the logic of someone as nice as Mr. Roudie wanting to spend time with Benetta if all she was doing was complaining, but if he wasn't going around telling people to avoid the bakery, it wasn't her business. Benetta seemed more interested in complaining about her lost seamstress shop, but Lillie vowed to avoid her from now on.

There was still, of course, the problem of the letter. Lillie pulled it from one of her drawers and scrutinized the writing as Kristin's words from earlier echoed in her mind.

"I know you think you've made a mess of things, but I've never known anyone to make such a mess that they couldn't be forgiven."

"I'm not going to be scared into feeling embarrassed about my past. And I'm certainly not leaving," Lillie announced as she tore up the letter. She paused, looking around the empty shop. "Unless, of course, no one comes to buy anything from me."

"Who are you talking to?"

Lillie spun around to find a short woman in the doorway. Her clothes looked like they'd been mended a few times, and her hair was pulled back in a white kerchief, so Lillie pegged her as one of the denizens of south Silverkeep.

"Oh, um. No one," Lillie said, quickly stashing the pieces of the letter in the nearby trash. "I'm Lillie. Can I help you?"

"My husband said he got something sweet from you yesterday," she said, following as Lillie scurried to the front counter.

"Who's your husband?"

"Paul Jacob," she said.

"Yes, and his brother Glen, right?" Lillie said, relaxing a little. "They're lovely."

"They're a mess and a half," she said with a hearty roll of her eyes. "Only married one, didn't think I was marrying the other, too. But as soon as we tied the knot, the other one moved into the small apartment next door and never left."

Lillie could certainly see how close they were. "Well, what can I do for you, Ms…?"

"Evangeline," she said. "Look, I don't know if you *do* this, but their birthday's coming up—"

"Do you want a birthday cake?" Lillie said with a gasp.

"Erm, yes." Evangeline stared at her, a little nervously. "Kristin Honeygold told me you make 'em."

"I do!" Lillie would have to kiss the farmer next time she saw her. A birthday cake would be a whole gold coin. "What flavor would you like?"

"I honestly don't know. I normally try to make 'em myself, but I'm not…" She looked around at the case of sweets. "I don't do much with baking. Give me a fish, and I can fry it seven ways from Sunday."

"Seems to be a common theme around here," Lillie said. "I can do pretty much whatever you like. A lemon drizzle cake, or a strawberry cake, or…"

"That sounds way too fancy," she said. "What about a simple chocolate cake?"

"What flavor icing?"

"No icing." She shook her head. "Just a chocolate cake."

Lillie thought for a moment. Her regular chocolate cake recipe was divine, but she scaled back the sweetness to account for the buttercream icing on top. But she had another recipe that would fit the bill perfectly.

"A chocolate pound cake sounds like it would do," she said. "Would you like one cake or two?"

"Oh, I'm sure they'll eat it together. They eat everything together." She made a face. "How much is it? Two gold coins? Three?"

Lillie swallowed her excitement and the urge to overcharge the woman. "Just one. When do you need it by?"

She put the gold coin on the counter. "Tonight, if you can. Is that all right? I've been by a few times since you opened, but…well, you don't look that busy, but you're never here, so—"

"I can handle it," Lillie said, before stopping short. Mr. Calcut hadn't been by with the cocoa powder yet. How often did the merchant come and go?

No matter, she'd figure it out.

"Great. I'll be by in a few hours." She smiled. "You really are going to make their day. It was all I heard last night, them raving about your goodies."

"I'm honored you thought of me," Lillie said. "And I promise, I'll have something delicious by the end of the day."

As soon as Evangeline left, Lillie took off her apron and headed up the hill. There was *one* other person in town who dealt with chocolate, and perhaps if she was *extra* kind, he might be able to spare a few tablespoons. She didn't need much, though she was grateful Kristin had dropped off those jugs of milk and eggs now.

The Globe Café loomed ahead, and Lillie plastered on a smile as she strolled through the front door. As predicted, there were customers at all the tables, each with a pastry and a cup of coffee. Lillie strode to the front, aware that there were a few more eyes on her than before. How many of them had spoken with Benetta? She vowed to hold her head up high anyway.

She walked right up to the front counter, where Julian was pouring hot water into a filter over a cup.

He looked up with a handsome smile that immediately soured. "What are *you* doing here? Here to eat more pastries and make faces?"

"I apologize once again," Lillie said, forcing her nicest smile. "You caught me at a bad time. I'd swallowed wrong."

"Oh, is that what happened?" He snorted. "Well? What do you want?"

Lillie cleared her throat. "I've come *humbly* asking if I might borrow half a cup of cocoa powder. I would be happy to repay you for it once Mr. Calcut brings me the shipment I've ordered. But I'm in a bit of a pinch and need the cocoa today."

He narrowed his gaze at her. "You mean

someone actually wants something from you?"

"Yes, as a matter of fact," Lillie said, once again wondering if *he'd* been the one to write the letter she no longer cared about. "Wouldn't you know it, but there's an entire population who lives south of the town square who want things like birthday cakes, muffins, and tartlets." She held her tongue rather than tell him that they'd been *un*welcome in his café. "One of them has put in a rush order for a birthday cake. Chocolate. But I'm all out of cocoa powder, so here I am."

"You know, we can do birthday cakes," he said. "Maybe you should send her up here if she's in such a rush. And you should go back to where you came from."

Lillie's patience evaporated as she took a threatening step toward him. "Now you *listen* here, you…" She grabbed hold of her temper before she really insulted him. "All I'm asking for is *half* a cup of cocoa powder. I'm *sure* you can spare it. I know Mr. Calcut was by yesterday, and based on the wide variety of goods in your case, you have plenty of different recipes you can choose from in the meantime."

Julian smiled humorlessly. "I'm terribly sorry, but I also have a chocolate cake order. I'll need all the cocoa powder I have on hand to—"

"Son, give her the cocoa powder. You have no such order, and if you do, you can tell them to delay their pickup another day."

Julian's entire body straightened as his father appeared at Lillie's shoulder. The elder Mr. Globe held a cup of coffee and gently sipped from the delicate rim, watching his son with a fierce expression. The younger Globe fidgeted like a teenager who'd disobeyed, and even though he was taller than his father, seemed to shrink in his presence.

"Don't make me repeat myself," Mr. Globe said, which sent a chill down even Lillie's spine.

Woodenly, Julian disappeared into the backroom.

"T-thank you," Lillie said. "I'm not sure… There's no need for the animosity."

"I quite agree." He placed the cup down on the counter and extended his hand. "You must be Lillie Dean. Audo Globe."

"Pleasure to meet you," Lillie said with a nervous smile as she shook his hand. "How did you know—"

"I know everyone in this town, except you," he said with a wry grin. "Besides that, the flour on your shirt gave you away."

Lillie looked down and laughed. "So it does."

"I wanted to let you know I'm *so* happy to have you in town," he said with a smile. "And I hope that my son's behavior doesn't deter you from doing business with me."

"N-not at all," Lillie said. "I mean...you're my landlord, so..."

"So I am."

Lillie couldn't read him. He said he was happy, but there was nothing behind his eyes that gave his thoughts away. "I'm not...aiming to be your son's competition."

"I don't think you will be. From what I understand, your skills far outmatch his." He smiled. "Keep up the good work. I'm rooting for you."

Before Lillie could respond, Julian appeared with a small box that he unceremoniously thrust into Lillie's hands without meeting his father's gaze. "I expect repayment," he said. "And don't make a habit of coming here, begging for ingredients. You manage your own shop, and I'll manage mine."

"I plan to," Lillie said firmly. "But know that if *you* ever need anything, *my* door is always open. I don't forget kindness, and you've been very kind to me today."

Julian bristled, as if the thought of being kind to Lillie made him want to pull his hair out.

"You know, these first few weeks of getting a business going can be so tough," Mr. Globe said, sipping his coffee again. "I remember when I first started out, I was taking loans from everyone I could to get my feet under me." He sighed. "Not that I'd expect you to understand that, Julian."

Julian shifted uncomfortably. "I started it—"

"With my money." Mr. Globe smiled, but there wasn't affection in it. "Not *quite* the same."

Lillie glanced between the two of them again, feeling like this was a conversation she desperately didn't want to be part of. "Well, I do have to get back to the bakery and make this cake. A-appreciate the cocoa, Julian." She turned to Audo. "Good day to you, Mr. Globe."

As a general rule, Lillie didn't want to get in the middle of family squabbles, but she couldn't help but ponder the dynamic between father and son. Clearly, Mr. Globe wasn't too happy with his son's café, but if that was the case, why give him the seed money, and more importantly, *why* had Lillie been allowed to move in? There was something missing there, but Lillie didn't want to spend more time thinking about the sour-faced café owner and his mysterious, rich father.

Instead, she started a fire in the oven and pulled out her large mixing bowls. The recipe required a pound each of sugar, butter, and flour. Five eggs, which effectively wiped out what Kristin had given her earlier in the day. A cup of milk, plus some leavening, salt, and a little whisper of magic.

As she had this morning, she started by making butter from the milk then creamed it with the sugar, adding eggs one at a time. In another bowl, she mixed together the dry ingredients, including six handfuls of cocoa then combined the wet and dry until the mixture was combined. Leaving that to sit for a moment, she looked through her baking pans until she found a unique tube pan, with a single hole in the middle. She rubbed butter along the outside of the pan and dusted it with cocoa powder, then added the mixture, checking the oven to make sure it was hot enough. Then she put the cake inside.

"Well, that's that," Lillie said, dusting off her hands. She took a moment to check her stock—she did have plenty of flour and sugar left. But she'd need more milk and eggs from Kristin, especially since she'd reached the end of her freshening spells for the pastries in front.

As soon as she pulled the chocolate cake from the oven, the front door opened, and three young women walked in—one of them wearing livery signaling she was a rich person's servant. They oohed and aahed over the goods as Lillie approached.

"Hey there," she said. "What can I get for you?"

"This all looks *amazing*," the livery-wearing girl said. "I heard from Sarah Watkins, who heard from Mary Zankman, who heard from Evangeline Jacob that I *had* to come here and see what you have."

Lillie recognized one of those names. "I'm glad to be recommended. I've got strawberry cupcakes down there, plus some blueberry scones left. And—oh, right! The chocolate chip cookies." She hadn't gotten around to putting the rest of them on display, so she ducked back into the kitchen and brought them out. "Just baked this morning."

"Oh, wow." The second girl, who had bright red hair and freckles, peered into the box. "I do love a chocolate chip cookie. They're so good right out of the oven."

Lillie hesitated. "I could…warm them up for you? With, erm." She took a breath. "With magic?"

The girls shared a look then giggled nervously. "If you're willing, I'm willing."

"Me too."

"Let's do it."

Lillie grinned as she told the cookies to warm up. Within seconds, steam rose from the plate, and the chocolate chunks took on a melty sort of gleam. The trio squealed and reached for them, cooing with delight as they realized they were, in fact, fresh-from-the-oven hot.

"Oh, my *goodness*," Livery-girl said. "This is *outrageous*!"

"The best cookie I've had in my life."

"What have we been missing? Eating food without magic all this time." The third girl, who had dark brown skin and a button nose, turned to Lillie with a bright smile. "I *demand* that you give me more of those." She reached into her pocket and placed a gold coin on the counter. "Now!"

"Oh, um…" Lillie cleared her throat. "Unfortunately, I'm fresh out. But I'm hopeful I'll run into Mr. Calcut soon so I can get more chocolate from him." She wasn't about to zip up to Julian's again to ask *him* for anything.

"Something smells divine," the redhead said, sniffing the air. "What do you have cooking?"

"A birthday cake for a customer," Lillie said.

"You do *birthday cakes* too?" The third girl squealed. "I'll have to put an order in for my cousin. Would you do a just-because cake?"

"Absolutely." Lillie loved these girls already. "I can do any sort of cake you can imagine."

"Would you make it magical?" She leaned in, as if they were sharing a secret. "You're willing to do that? Even with—"

"There's no need to hide magic anymore," Lillie said. "If you want magic, I'll put it in the cake."

The girls promised they'd be back soon, but took a gold's worth of pastries with them, talking animatedly to each other. Lillie put their coin with the rest of her money. Between the excitable girls and Evangeline, she was starting to add to her collection instead of constantly spending it. A good trend.

But Lillie's lucrative day ended there. Other than Evangeline, who came at four to pick up the cake and was overjoyed at the sight, smell, and *weight* of it, no one else came to the shop. Still, as morose as Lillie had been this morning, she was certainly feeling much better about her future in Silverkeep. She tidied the shop, grabbed two scones to eat with dinner, as she was all out of rosemary bread, then headed up the stairs.

But before she could walk into her apartment, the door across the hall opened, and Ursil walked out, looking ashen.

"Oh, Ursil," Lillie said. "What's wrong?"

"Kristin told me about that letter you got," he said.

Lillie's heart sputtered. Perhaps she'd been too hasty. "Yes? What about it?"

But instead of berating her, or telling her to leave, or all the other horrible things she was imagining, he merely reached into his pocket and handed her a piece of paper. To Lillie's surprise, there was almost *identical* writing on it.

Leave Silverkeep or I'll tell all your fishermen buddies about your wife's cheating ways.

Chapter Ten

"Cheating?" Lillie said, looking up at him. Nikola didn't seem like the kind of person to be unfaithful in a marriage, and the couple doted on each other. "What is—"

"Not *that* kind," Ursil said with a laugh that didn't quite reach his eyes. "Cheatin' out on the water. Gettin' more fish than is normal. Is natural. Is…"

"Non-magical?" Lillie thought for a moment. "Nikola."

"Yeah, I'm a garden-variety human," he said, rubbing his stomach with a muted smile. "My wife, though... She's got nymph blood in her. Not enough to be flagged by the queen's folk, or they would've taken her like they did everyone else. But enough that she's got a sixth sense for where to find the fish around here. She's never had a bad day on the water."

"I fail to see how that's worth writing a letter about," Lillie said. Then again, she'd also been overly worried about *her* secrets getting out.

He opened and closed his mouth. "Suppose you haven't heard about the Fisherfolk Council, have you?"

Lillie shook her head.

"It's kinda what it sounds like. A group of folks who manage who gets slips on the docks, and who doesn't. They say it's a neutral process, but we all know it's political. There's an election for who gets votes on it, and it's the same pea brains every year. They got their friends, who always get a slip, then the rest of us gotta fight for whatever's left." He cleared his throat. "Since Nik's always got fish comin' in, and payin' the dockmaster, they give us a spot pretty much every year we've asked for it. But it always makes those who don't get one jealous."

"What do they do if they don't get a spot?" Lillie asked. "Just not fish?"

"Some do other jobs, workin' as dockhands to load and unload carts. But gettin' to be your own boss, that's what everyone wants. Gettin' up when you want and goin' out and catchin' as much as you can. That's the life."

"Why don't they build new docks that can fit everybody?" Lillie asked.

"We ain't got the room," he said. "The big ships bring in all the money, so they get the lion's share of space at the wharf. What's left is for us. Not to mention, there's a finite amount of fish here. If we let everyone out to cast their nets, we wouldn't have any left."

Lillie nodded. "So if the other fisherfolk found out that Nikola's ability was due to magic, instead of skill, they'd take away her fishing spot?"

"The McTavishes would, for sure. They've always been leery of her, thinkin' maybe she's got somethin'."

Lillie had briefly met the McTavishes when she'd brought her apology cookies to Mr. Roudie. "Why would they care?"

"They're the heads of the Fisherfolk Council. Been there since the purge, as, well, they were the only ones left. The rest of the folks, like us, trickled in. Some folks switched careers from dockhands to fisherfolk. Others, like Nik and myself, got invited to move here by Mr. Abora."

Lillie started. "He recruited you, too?"

"Right after the queen's folks came through, the place was even more of a ghost town than it is now," Ursil said. "We were some of the first to settle, and the rest of 'em showed up later."

"Hm." Lillie pursed her lips. "Who do you think would have the most to gain from Nikola no longer having a slip?"

"Jarvis Collin, for sure. Probably his friends Hipolita Tokely and Keegan Curtis, and definitely Lawson Dritter, too. I know they've been lookin' for a reason to take our spot away from us, especially since Jarvis lost his spot last year. Nik can't bring a net full of fish up the wharf without him sayin' somethin' about it."

"Definitely a motive," Lillie said. "Do you think you could convince them to come to the bakery? I might be able to find out something while they're enjoying a sweet treat." She certainly *wouldn't* be adding any truth-telling components to her confections this time. "Not that I'm trying to take advantage of the situation, but it does make a convenient meeting spot."

"If you want to take advantage, you go right ahead," he said. "You gotta make your money so you can keep bakin' for me."

"Is there anything happening that might've caused them to send the letter now?" Lillie asked.

"I can't think of anything. The Fisherfolk Council elections happen in the fall, and that's months away."

Lillie nodded. "Does anyone know her secret other than you?"

He shook his head. "I don't think anyone back in her old town knew, either. Kinda a family secret, you know? She only told me when we got hitched."

"Well, whoever knows her secret seems to know mine, too," Lillie said, tapping the letter on her hands.

"But I mean... You aren't hiding your magic," he said.

"The secret they have isn't about that," Lillie said with a wry grin.

"Oh? Then what is it?"

"I'd rather not say, if we're being honest," Lillie said, her cheeks warming. "I did something in my past I'm not proud of, and I learned my lesson. Which is why I'm not sure the person writing the letter is trying to nab your spot at the dock. What could they have to gain by threatening me?" She shook her head. "Do you think someone's trying to get us to leave this property? It doesn't seem coincidental we both live here, and both got letters."

"I mean, shouldn't they be talking with Mr. Globe?" Ursil said. "He's the landlord, ain't he?"

Lillie nodded. "There was a whole crowd of people up in the town square the other day angry with him for taking their property while they were in hiding. I wonder if our letter-writer is the old owner of our building." She put her hands to her hips. "The library would have records going back to before the war, wouldn't it?"

"You really think it's about that and not... erm..." He cleared his throat. "Your being open about magic? Maybe whoever sent the letter is angry about magical people."

"They're about to be in for a rude awakening," Lillie said. "I still think it's worthwhile to ask the archivist who lived here before we did, and whether we should expect them back. But I'm happy to meet with the fisherfolk, too. We'll figure this out, Ursil, I promise."

He smiled brightly at her. "I'm so glad you've moved in next door. I wouldn't know the first thing to do if I was doing this by myself."

"You have Nikola, don't you?"

"I haven't told her," he said. "Hid it from her as soon as I read it. She... Well, I know she'd be halfway to packing up and leaving if she knew. But I don't think that's fair. She shouldn't be punished for who she is—same as you shouldn't be punished for who *you* are."

Lillie's heart warmed. "Leave this with me. I'll get to the bottom of it."

The next morning, Lillie started her day by gathering all her ingredients and making an epic list of things to bake. If she was to be playing both host and interrogator to a group of fisherfolk, she wanted to put her best foot forward. She also wanted to meet with the archivist and didn't want to arrive empty-handed, in case there was some wheel-greasing to be done. Unfortunately, she'd used all her milk and eggs in the Jacobs's cake the day before. Clearly, she'd have to buy double from Kristin if she didn't want to be in this situation every morning.

Still, she found herself looking forward to the dairy farmer's arrival more than usual and purposefully didn't make anything sweet for her, so she'd have an excuse to keep her around longer. Kristin seemed to know more than anyone else about the scuttlebutt at the wharf, and Lillie had a hunch she'd not only corroborate, but *elaborate* on what Ursil had told her.

After Lillie had finished her baking list, she started on a list of questions for Kristin about the Fisherfolk Council. As she worked through it, she was…well, not relieved that Ursil had received a letter. But somehow finding the writer seemed less self-serving and more noble. The Kovens had been nothing but kind and generous to Lillie, especially Ursil, and the thought of them leaving filled her with such righteous anger, she might burn down the entire wharf with it. This, perhaps, was why Bev always found herself solving these problems. It felt good to help people who deserved it.

At six o'clock exactly, Kristin let herself into the kitchen, carrying a crate of milk and eggs, then predictably scowled. "Well? Where's my goodie?"

"Unfortunately, I'm all out of the very thing you've delivered," Lillie said, gently taking the crate from her. "If you give me fifteen minutes, I can whip up a scone for you. How about that?"

"I suppose I have fifteen minutes," Kristin said, walking over to sit on the kitchen stool. "I take it business is good, then? If you don't have any milk or eggs left from yesterday."

"I've made a few sales, yes," Lillie said, pouring the first jug of milk into a bowl and setting it to whip itself up. "But I'm expecting a big crowd today. I hope." She liked Kristin but didn't trust the loquacious dairy farmer to keep Nikola's secret. "Can I double my order for tomorrow?"

"Golly." Kristin gasped as the milk frothed. "I've never seen anything like that before. What are you doing to it?"

"Making butter," Lillie said with a smile. "Faster to do it this way than to sit and churn it."

"You aren't lying. I've got blisters from doing it at my house." She inspected the bowl closely, watching the solids separate. "Forget paying me. I'll get a pound of butter from you on my way home. Would be amazing to never have to churn it again."

"Sold," Lillie said. Then, sensing she had Kristin's attention, she asked, "What do you know about the Fisherman's Council?"

"It's a bunch of connected blowhards," Kristin said, her attention still on the bowl. "The

McTavishes run it. They meet once a year to divvy up the slips down at the docks. They say it's in the interest of fairness, but if you ask me, it's all about who pays the most for the privilege."

"Does Nikola Koven pay for hers?" Lillie asked.

"Oh, she's one of those who gets in on *merit*," Kristin said. "She always brings in the most fish, which means she pays the most to the dockmaster—that would be Mr. Globe—so he always votes for her to stay."

"He does have a stake in everything in this town, doesn't he?" Lillie muttered as the bowl containing the butter came to a stop. As Kristin watched wordlessly, Lillie separated the butter and put it into the bowl where the flour, sugar, salt, and leavening were waiting. Once again, she set the bowl to spin, the flour churning on itself, breaking up the butter into pebble-sized quantities. To that, Lillie added milk and mixed until a dough came together.

"Hm." Lillie put her hand on her hip.

"What's wrong?" Kristin asked.

"I made blueberry scones earlier this week," Lillie said, walking to the crates of produce. She pawed through what she had, and nothing spoke to her as a good mix-in for a scone. "Maybe I can spare some of those chocolate chips. Mr. Calcut should be bringing me more soon."

"Now, there's an idea," Kristin said excitedly.

As Lillie mixed in the chocolate chips, making

sure to keep some for the batch of cookies later, she returned to the topic at hand. "So how do all the other fisherfolk feel about magic? Does anyone have a real strong objection to it?"

"What, like your magic? They don't mind it, as far as I've heard."

"I meant fisherfolk with magic. Maybe there's a selkie or something in the bunch. Would that upset things?"

"For *sure*. The McTavishes, they're strictly anti-magic when it comes to fishing."

Lillie dumped the dough clump out onto the table and formed it into two identically sized rounds. "They haven't been in my shop yet, either."

"Why?" Kristin circled the table. "Did you get another letter?"

"No, I didn't," Lillie said then smiled as she sliced the rounds into triangles and placed them on the baking sheet. She opted to keep the Kovens' letter close to the vest to narrow the list of suspects. "Just trying to get the lay of the land and know who I should avoid."

"Other than Julian Globe, I don't think anyone else around here is too worried about you," she said. "Speaking of, I heard from Ash Keedling, who heard from Inez Berrington, that you went back to his café yesterday."

"I needed some cocoa powder," Lillie said, walking the scones to the oven. She stood in front of the open oven for a minute, convincing the dough to cook a little faster so Kristin could get on her way. "Evangeline Jacob purchased a chocolate cake for her husband and his brother."

"Ah."

"Was it that big of a scene?" Lillie asked with a small laugh. "Though, his father was there, so maybe." She tapped her finger on the table. "What's their story, anyway?"

"Who? The Globes? Just rich and entitled."

"Yes, but... Mr. Globe, the elder one, told me I was a much better baker than his son, and that he was *rooting* for me. But he'd also given Julian the money to start his bakery." Lillie shouldn't have been gossiping about family squabbles, but she couldn't help her curiosity. "Why is he rooting for... well, I hate to say it, but his son's direct competition?"

"No clue," Kristin said. "I try to avoid thinking about the Globes as much as possible."

"Right. Sorry. After the welcome I received from Julian, I should probably follow suit. But desperate times, you know? I *really* needed that cocoa powder yesterday." She paused. "How often is Mr. Calcut in town, anyway?"

"Who knows? I don't keep track of him. He appears like the wind and disappears." Kristin made a spooky noise. "But I'm sure he'd probably hear if you needed him. He's creepy like that."

"Hopefully, he makes an appearance today, because I'd like to avoid another scene at Globe Café," Lillie said. "But speaking of the town square, what time does the library open?"

"Nine, I think." Kristin frowned. "Why? Looking to get a good read?"

"Actually, I wanted to know who lived here before me," Lillie said. "Ursil said he didn't know."

"Why does it matter?"

"Lots of folks are appearing out of the woodwork, demanding their old property back," Lillie said. "I'm not sure whoever wrote me that letter wasn't the old owner." She glanced at Kristin. "Do you know?"

"Nah. I only started coming to town without my sister about three years ago," she said. "I'm sure the librarian would know."

"Let's hope." Lillie pulled the scones from the oven, pleased that they'd turned out perfect. She encouraged the heat to dissipate enough that she could pick one up off the pan and hand it to Kristin. "As promised: one chocolate chip scone. Thank you *so* much for your patience."

Chapter Eleven

Kristin ended up taking two scones—mostly because she inhaled the first before she'd even walked out the door—and promised to be back on her way home to pick up some butter. Lillie really was getting the better end of the stick, as it was no trouble at all to make it.

Still, Lillie really did hope Mr. Calcut came back today, because she only had enough chocolate left to make half a dozen cookies, should the girls from the day before come back. They were, of course, welcome to the chocolate chip scones, but they weren't quite as sweet and melty as the cookies.

She spent the rest of the morning baking peach muffins, raspberry-jam-filled tartlets (with quite the crisp bottom, thank you very much), and chocolate cupcakes using the very last of her cocoa powder. Those she iced with buttercream and topped with a single slice of strawberry, using what she had left, and she boxed one up to bring to the librarian.

At a quarter to nine, Lillie locked up the shop. Ursil wouldn't be down for another hour, and she had plenty of time to get back. But she still left a note stuck in the door window telling him she'd be back at ten, in case he arrived early.

The library was a beautiful brick building right next to the town hall, with one dark wooden door and a pair of windows in the front. Lillie purposefully ignored the nearby Globe Café and the patrons who might've noticed her in the town square. She was starting to get the feeling she wasn't *allowed* on this side of town, which was silly. She could go anywhere she pleased. But the feeling remained.

Ignoring it, she turned the knob and walked into the library as the town hall clock chimed nine. She craned her neck at the tall shelves of books that met her, trying to count them. Everything was impeccably clean, and each book on the shelf was organized by size. She peered into a nearby stack, reading the names of the titles. There seemed to be a nice selection of fiction. Lillie did love to read, though she'd had to leave all her books behind in Lower Pigsend. She'd been so busy getting the bakery ready that she hadn't even thought about—

"Can I help you?"

The voice startled her, nearly causing her to drop the cupcake box, and it didn't sound pleasant at all. Lillie spun to smile at a young man with short black hair and a permanent scowl that could've given Julian Globe's a run for its money. He surveyed her with more than a little disdain and shifted the three books he was holding in his arms.

"Hi," Lillie said. "I'm—"

"I know who you are. Lillie Dean. Pobyd. Live down south. What do you want?"

Lillie frowned. This was certainly not the kind, sweet librarian she was used to. But perhaps with chocolate, he might come around. "I actually had a question I was hoping you could answer."

"I *probably* can." He *thunked* the books down then noticed the box in her hand. "What is *that*?"

"Oh! A gift." Lillie brought the box forward and opened it.

The librarian recoiled in horror. "*No food or drink in the library!*"

She pulled the box back toward herself. "S-sorry. I thought—"

"And I'm allergic to chocolate," he said with a sneer.

"Good to know." Lillie quickly put the top back

on and hid the offending item under her arm, as if it might escape and bite the librarian.

He didn't seem to appreciate the gesture. "What's your question?"

"Can you tell me who owned my bakery before the war?" Lillie asked, keeping her tone light and friendly. "And, more importantly, what happened to them?"

His nostrils flared. "I can tell you who owned it, but as to what happened to them, I'm afraid that information is *probably* unknown to me. I'm not responsible for keeping track of everyone who was arrested by the queen—if that's what happened."

"Right." She shifted. "Well, the name, then."

He disappeared and came back moments later with a large book, which he blew dust off, right into Lillie's face, earning a sneeze from the pobyd.

He glared at her. "Cover your mouth."

"Sorry," Lillie said, juggling the box as she sniffed. "Wasn't expecting—"

He slammed open the book, flipping the pages. "Let's see. You're on the southern part of Main Street."

"Yes, a block up from the docks," Lillie said, wishing she had something to wipe her nose with. She didn't *dare* ask the librarian for anything.

"Hm." He flipped through the pages then stopped and ran his finger down a list of names. "Huh."

"Huh what?" Lillie's heart thudded.

"This says it was owned by a Reynard Moussison." He gave her a look, as if this were somehow her fault. "I've never heard of him."

"Were you here before—"

"*No.*" He slammed the book shut. "Can I help you with anything else? If not, please take your *baked good* out of the library before you leave crumbs everywhere, and I have to spend *all day* cleaning it up."

Lillie left the library quickly, not wanting to feel the librarian's wrath any more than she already had. She had a name, which was a good start. The next thing would be to check Mr. Abora's handy list to see if there was anyone matching the last name *Moussison*. She checked the time (a little past nine) and decided she could dash in and chat with Mr. Abora about it.

Unfortunately, when she walked into the town hall, she found an even *larger* crowd than the day before waiting to speak to him. They were once again broken up into factions, with the clearly magical returners on the left and the clearly non-magical current residents on the right. Mr. Abora's door was shut, as were the mayor's and the sheriff's.

Lillie approached one of the two magical folks sitting closest to her. One, a bored-looking woman with green hair, toyed with an emerald lock, while the other, a blue-skinned, thin man, seemed furious. "Is there still a sign-up sheet?"

He pointed to the table at the front of the room.

"Thank you," Lillie said with a kind smile. "Erm." She offered him the cupcake the librarian had declined. "Cupcake? I've opened a bakery in town."

"Ooh, yes please." The green-haired woman snatched the box and gasped when she opened it. "Oh, how delightful! We'll have to stop by."

"When we get our home back," her partner said with a growl. "Do me a favor and check how many names are in front of Greeley Sloos."

"Will do," Lillie said, sauntering up to the front. She found the sign-up sheet, looking for similar handwriting to the letters, but didn't see anything that looked close—nor did anyone have the last name Moussison. Helpfully, Mr. Abora had them list where they'd come from, and most listed *Lower Silverkeep*, which Lillie had to guess was a similar set-up to Lower Pigsend.

As Lillie was examining the names, Mr. Abora's door opened, and a pair of scowling women exited —one with bright purple curls, and the other with pale ivory skin. Mr. Abora followed, walking up to the table where Lillie stood.

"How's it going?" Lillie asked.

"Well, until we figure out exactly who's still out there... I'm afraid we're at something of a standstill," he said, looking out at the crowd. "Don't tell me there are *more* people? Goodness, they keep coming, don't they?"

"It certainly—"

"Hey!" an angry voice called from behind them. "Why does she get to talk with you before I do?"

"I've been waiting here for three hours!"

"I've been here since yesterday!"

"Erm, excuse me," Mr. Abora said, snatching the list from Lillie. "Yes, sorry. Erm. Mr. Sloos? Are you here?"

The blue-skinned man and his green-haired partner rose and walked toward the office. Mr. Abora held open the door and ushered them in then closed it behind him.

A murmur of discussion erupted in the room, especially around the duo who'd emerged. Lillie strained to listen, catching some derogatory phrases about Mr. Abora, while also understanding there was no resolution that either party liked.

"Have to give up *half* my client list," the non-magical person said, crossing her arms over her chest. "I built that client list!"

"On my business!" the magical person bellowed from across the room. "You're lucky that's all you have to give up. Now I gotta open shop down by the smelly docks!"

"Serves you right, coming back into town," another barked. "The queen did us all a favor, clearing you lot out."

Angry shouts erupted from the group, and Lillie looked around for Sheriff Juno, but she still seemed to be gone on her trip.

Instead, Mr. Abora's door opened, and he appeared, red-faced and furious. "Quiet down, or I'll cancel all your appointments!"

The threat seemed to work, and the arguments lost their ferocity, though the grumbling and dirty looks continued.

Lillie glanced at the clock; she needed to get back to the bakery. She'd hoped to have better news about Mr. Moussison, but if he was in town, he hadn't made it to the town hall yet, or at least, hadn't put his name down.

She was already halfway out the door when a sneering voice called out, "What are *you* doing here?"

Benetta sat on the edge of one of the benches on the magical side, fanning herself and wearing an extravagant hat.

"Benetta, hello," Lillie said, hoping this conversation would be short. "Just here to… Well, I had a question for Mr. Abora. But I've got to get back to the bakery, so—"

"Hmph. Off to sell more *salted* cookies." She lifted her nose higher. "Or whatever was really wrong with them. Can't believe you'd trick poor Roudie like that. He's a simple creature, you know."

Lillie pursed her lips at the other woman then crossed the row to sit next to her. Benetta jumped back, clearly not expecting Lillie to come so close, and held her fan ready to defend herself.

"Put down your fan. I come in peace." Lillie cleared her throat. "And I want to know who you've told about Lower Pigsend."

"I'm sorry?" Benetta blinked at her.

"I received a letter," Lillie said. "One that said if I didn't leave town, they'd reveal my secret to…well, everyone. Seeing as you're the only one in Silverkeep who knows my secret, you're my number one suspect. So…" Lillie smiled. "Who've you told?"

Benetta waited, examining her fan closely and seeming to milk the pause for all it was worth. "No one."

Lillie blinked. "What?"

"I haven't told a single person about your sordid little past," Benetta said. "Not even poor Roudie, who I'm sure would be keen to hear it." She pursed her lips. "You see, we've all got much bigger problems to contend with right now. Our property's been unfairly usurped by that monstrous Audo Globe, and it seems we'll all have to fight to get it back." She shifted uncomfortably. "The *gall* of him. My many-times-great grandfather *built* half this city, and I'll be darned if I don't reclaim what's rightfully mine."

Lillie believed her, if only because she didn't see

why Benetta would lie about that.

Mr. Abora emerged, and the green-haired woman joined her partner in frustration. "Where are we supposed to sleep? The Silverkeep Inn is booked solid."

"I'm working on that," Mr. Abora said, snatching the paper. "Mrs. Featherswift?"

A creature with large, white feathered wings rose and walked toward his office, leaving a trail of down behind her. Mr. Abora made a face as she ducked under the doorframe then slammed the door behind him.

"Goodness, can you imagine trying to hide those from the queen's soldiers?" Benetta said with a laugh.

"Why are you still here?" Lillie asked. "Haven't you met with Mr. Abora already?"

"His offer left much to be desired," she said. "He seems to think I have *no* claim to my property. He said Mr. Globe would be *happy* to find an alternate location for me, at the cost of twelve gold pieces a month for a shopfront and apartment." She sniffed. "Going from owning my entire building outright to having to *pay* that greedy merchant *twelve* gold pieces a month while he collects money from a tenant squatting in *my* home."

"What else can you do?" Lillie asked.

"I'm going to keep pressing the matter," Benetta said, shifting on her seat. "There are at least twenty of us in this same situation now. One voice might not sway a man like Audo Globe, but twenty might, especially as they were only down the road in Lower Silverkeep."

"Was that like—"

"Less barbaric, of course," Benetta said. "They didn't have to deal with the lack of fresh fruit and flour nonsense—but they still suffered." She licked her lips. "Still, I don't see *quite* as many familiar faces as I'd hoped. Too many people *were* actually caught by the queen."

She cast a sad look around her side of things, and Lillie realized another reason for Benetta wanting to stick around. This had turned into a meeting point for all the returning creatures, mostly so they could get their property back, but also to find their lost friends and relations. Lillie didn't have anyone back in Sheepsburg who would be waiting for her, but she could empathize.

"Who are you waiting for?" Lillie asked.

Benetta moved like she was about to sneer at Lillie again, but instead she shook her head. "My sister. She's like me, skilled with the needle in a magical way. I was…away from the city when the queen's people came through. In Middleburg to meet with a new fabric vendor. Was able to find my way down to Lower Pigsend before it closed." She adjusted her skirts again. "I hope she was able to find a safe place, but…" She cleared her throat again, this time sounding like she had a lump of emotion there. "None of the folks in Lower Silverkeep I've spoken to have heard of her."

"Don't give up hope," Lillie said softly. "There must've been little pockets all over the country like Lower Pigsend. She might've escaped to one of those, you know?"

Benetta met her smiling gaze with a glare. "Let's hope there weren't any treacherous pobyds down *there* to ruin everything."

Chapter Twelve

"Moussison? Can't say I've ever heard of him."

Ursil was waiting for Lillie when she returned to the bakery, chastising her for leaving when there could be paying customers yet again. She apologized, telling him where she'd been and what she'd found out from the library, and that softened his attitude a little.

"The librarian didn't give me much, either," Lillie said. "He's quite rude. Gives Julian Globe a run for his money."

"Sexton? Yeah, he's a piece of work," Ursil said. "Always got something twistin' his britches. Pay him no mind. None of us do."

"I can see why he'd take a job where he didn't have to speak much with people."

"Oh, he speaks with us plenty," Ursil said with a laugh. "We gotta provide him with our yearly catch amounts for the town almanac. It's not my *favorite* time of year, I'll tell you that."

"I didn't see Moussison's name on the list of folks trying to speak with Mr. Abora," Lillie said. "That doesn't mean he's not in town, though. And if he's the one trying to get us to leave through nasty letters, then he might not even need to speak to Mr. Globe."

"I'll ask Nik about it, and ask around at the wharf. If he was some hoity-toity property owner, I'm sure someone has heard of him. Now!" He finished off the last bite of cupcake. "Are you ready to interrogate the fisherfolk?"

Lillie nodded. She still didn't think the fisherfolk were behind the letters, as she couldn't really say why they'd have a grudge against her. But Ursil seemed convinced of it, and Lillie was willing to play along, if only to learn more about her wharf neighbors.

"I'm gonna badger as many of 'em as I can to come see you," he said. "But you'll really want to focus on Jarvis Collin and the McTavishes. They're really the ones who've had it out for us." He glanced into her shop. "Do you have anything in there that could, I don't know, force 'em to talk about stuff they don't want to?"

Lillie did, in fact, have some jam (she'd decided against throwing it out, and it was currently hiding in the back of one of her shelves, labeled *Do Not Use*), but she didn't feel comfortable using it on people who might potentially become customers.

"Not today," Lillie said. "I've got what you see here. Need Mr. Calcut to come back with more chocolate, though. Might as well put my order in for some more flour and sugar, too, if he's going to be this long between visits."

"He's a creepy one," Ursil said with a shiver. "I know Kristin likes him. I think she finds him intriguing, like she finds most odd things in the world. But the way he moves, and how he gets things outta nowhere..." He shivered. "You be careful."

"I'm in a business arrangement with him," Lillie said. "I can't possibly be a bakery without chocolate, now can I? Julian Globe made himself *quite* clear that I'm not to darken his door in search of help."

Ursil left after that, promising he'd send the fisherfolk after lunch. Lillie hovered around the front window, adjusting and shifting the display plates then shifting them back. She really wasn't meant to be this idle, but without paying customers, she didn't want to head into the kitchen to make anything.

A few minutes after noon, the first round of fisherfolk arrived—Jarvis Collin and Lawson Dritter. They looked sunburnt and windswept, like they'd come off the water, and inspected the goods in both the window and display case, unable to make up their minds. Lillie recognized Jarvis as the fishmonger who'd accosted Nikola the first time she'd been to the market.

"Ursil went on and on," Jarvis said, leaning over the display case. "Just came down here to shut him up, to be honest."

Lillie let that roll off her back. "Well, I'm so happy to have you check out my shop. I'm delighted to be on this side of town. Not much else around here, is there?"

"Everyone with any sense moved up north," Lawson said. "But I'm sure the Globes lobbied to put you down here in the sticks."

"Do you two live up north?" Lillie asked.

Jarvis nodded, while Lawson shook his head. "I live on my boat."

"Your boat?" Lillie couldn't believe that was possible—but it piqued her interest. Someone who physically needed a slip to get off their boat might be tempted to send nasty letters to the Kovens. "How do you manage that?"

"Got a hammock in the hull," he said. "Mine's a bit bigger than the rest of 'em. I'm sure you've seen it out there."

Jarvis rolled his eyes. "It's not *that* much bigger. And Lawson's a cheapskate. He makes enough for ten dock slips. Only person who catches more fish is Nikola."

"One day, I'll catch up with her," he said with a wink.

"Did you end up finding where she was catching those red fish?" Lillie asked.

Jarvis gave her a sideways glance. "Eh?"

"The other day, you asked her where she'd found those red fish, I think they were?" She flashed an innocent smile. "I confess, I have no idea what kind of fish is what, but it sounds like red fish are…in demand?"

"I'll say," Lawson said. "The northern folk—Mr. Globe and his friends, in particular—are obsessed with them. Pay through the nose, too. But the past two or three weeks, only person who's been able to find them has been Nikola Koven."

"I think she's up to no good," Jarvis said. "Something off about her, you know?"

"You think?" Lillie asked. "She seems nice enough to me."

"You don't catch that many fish without having something up your sleeve," he said, looking around. "You probably know more than me, being magical yourself. Has she got the spirit in her?"

"Spirit?" Lillie chuckled. "You mean, is she magical? I can't say I can tell. But if she were magical, wouldn't she have been arrested?"

"Lots of folks gave the queen the slip," Lawson said. "Including yourself."

Lillie smiled. "I found safe haven for a few years."

She held her breath, waiting for either man to mention Lower Pigsend. Not that it meant anything, but if they knew where Lillie was from, maybe they'd been behind the letters.

"Where'd you find safe haven from the queen?" Jarvis asked, dubiously. "No, I'm sure you got lucky."

"Yeah, or the queen's people thought you weren't a threat," Lawson said. "Who'd have anything to fear from a baker? You're going to chocolate them to death?"

Lillie opened her mouth to tell them a story about a pobyd of lore who had, in fact, poisoned a queen, but she thought better of it. Neither man seemed to know anything about Lower Pigsend *or* her past, and neither seemed smart enough to pull off lying that well.

"Well, I don't know about that, but my chocolate cupcakes *are* divine," she said, gesturing to the case. "And quite addictive, if you ask Ursil."

~

The second group arrived much like the first, telling Lillie they'd been strong-armed into making an appearance. They didn't seem quite as competitive with Nikola, though, and were a bit more enthusiastic about tasting the tartlets and scones. Still, Lillie didn't glean much more from them than she had the other two. Nikola was the best, they all thought something was up, but no one really knew exactly what—and neither person knew anything about Lillie's hijinks in Lower Pigsend.

Finally, Jan and Orxan McTavish walked into the shop, taking up more space than either of the previous four as their voices boomed. From what Ursil and Kristin had told her, the couple took turns fishing and mongering, depending on the day, and were equally good at both. They had been the only fisherfolk left behind after the purge, and, like Mr. Globe, had taken advantage of that to build their power structure. They, of course, had the closest slip in the wharf, and the prime location to sell their fish, and the final say who stayed on the Fisherfolk Council and who left.

Ursil had also been correct that Jan, at least, wasn't comfortable with magic. Their partner Orxan lingered over the case and asked questions about each pastry and how she made them, but Jan kept their distance, arms folded as if a chocolate scone would jump out of the display case and bite them.

"I've always loved the idea of baking," Orxan said. "But never did have the time to learn how to do it. Seems quite scientific to me. Have you always been a baker?"

"Come by it naturally," Lillie said, gesturing to the window, where *Pobyd Perfections* had been painted on. She didn't want to make Jan more uncomfortable, but the conversation needed to be had. "Both my parents were pobyds, too."

Jan made a face, lingering near the door. "Awfully brave of you, announcing it to the world like that. Hope Her Majesty's soldiers don't come through town and steal you away."

"Her Majesty has been defeated," Lillie said. "She's no longer in power."

"I don't believe that," Jan said. "Things were finally settling down, you know? We'd cleared out all the magical nonsense—no offense—and the world was getting on with it. Now you tell me all that's about to be turned on its head?"

Lillie lifted a shoulder. "One could say it wasn't much better when the queen was in power, especially for those of us on the wrong side of her edicts."

"Yeah? And where were you during this time that you *avoided* those edicts?" Jan asked.

Interesting. Was Jan trying to get Lillie to say the name Lower Pigsend? Lillie opened and closed her mouth, unsure which angle she wanted to go with. Finally, she said, "You haven't heard?"

"All I know is you showed up here three weeks ago with two old folks, set up your bakery, and Ursil Koven can't stop talking about you," Jan said. "I did hear something about you coming from the north, though."

"Pigsend," Lillie said. "Small farming village near Middleburg. Lovely place. Amazing Harvest Festival in the fall."

"And the queen just...ignored you there?"

"I wasn't advertising my magical abilities when I lived in Pigsend," Lillie said, veering closer to the subject she wanted to broach. If she could catch someone admitting they knew she'd been in Lower Pigsend, she'd find her culprit. "But I spent a few years in another, safer place beforehand."

"If it was so safe, why did you leave?"

Lillie met Jan's gaze, scrutinizing the fisherfolk for some hint of what they were getting at. "Because while safe, it wasn't fulfilling. Left a lot to be desired." She brightened. "Still, it doesn't matter now. I've moved to Silverkeep, the queen and her laws are no more, and I'm quite happy about all of it."

Jan snorted, but Orxan put a hand on their shoulder. "Leave the girl alone, Jan. No need to discuss politics. You do that enough at the council."

"Council?" Lillie feigned ignorance. "Like a city council?"

"Fisherfolk Council," Orxan said. "Jan and I run it—have for the last few years, with Mr. Globe's blessing, of course. The Silverkeep government has their hands full with all the big ships at the docks, keeping the rich merchants happy. They gave us an allotment of dock slips, I'm sure you've seen them."

Lillie nodded.

"Well, we got more fisherfolk than slips, so we have to use a lottery system to make sure we're divvying them up fairly."

"So you draw names out of a hat?" That wasn't Lillie's understanding.

"Not exactly," Jan said, giving their partner a look. "Obviously, Mr. Globe won't get paid if we only give slips out to folks who aren't the most productive. So we give priority to certain people."

"Like Nikola," Lillie said, searching their faces for a reaction.

"Yeah, like Nikola." A flash of annoyance passed over Orxan's face, but Jan didn't share it. "They're your neighbors, so I won't speak ill of them, but Nikola seems to have some kinda good spirit looking after her. She always comes in with more fish than she can fit on her boat, even when the rest of us are barely finding anything."

"One would think you'd follow her to find where the fish are," Lillie suggested.

"That's against the code," Jan said. "We've all got our spots and our methods, and we don't poach from each other. Fisherfolk are very proud people, and we don't like cheaters."

Lillie looked up at Jan, who spoke while looking out the window. *Cheaters?* Ursil's letter had insinuated Nikola was cheating. Was it coincidence that the fisherfolk used the same language?

"Well, there's no cheating here," Lillie said, after a moment's pause. "Just delicious cupcakes and other confections. Can I interest you in anything?"

"Did you use magic to make them?" Jan asked.

The way they phrased the question, Lillie feared the rumor mill about her spiking Benetta's cookies with magic had started. She chose her words carefully.

"A little bit of magic slips into everything I bake," Lillie said. "I can remove it, if it bothers you. All it does is enhance the flavors and make it more delicious."

"Oh, come on, Janny, that's harmless," Orxan said. "No need to worry about a little taste—"

"I'll pass," Jan said with a hard look. "Come, Orxan, we have to get back to the market. We've got fish to sell."

"Are you sure I can't—"

"No, thank you," Jan said, already halfway out the door. But they weren't all the way through before they stopped short, all the blood draining from their face.

Mr. Calcut slipped by them through the open door, smiling their toothy, mysterious smile at the fisherfolk. "Jan, you're looking well."

"A-ah, Mr. Calcut," Jan said, looking more nervous than they should have. "N-nice to see you again. What are you doing here?"

Mr. Calcut lifted a canvas bag. "Delivering goods to Ms. Dean, of course."

"Right." Jan shifted, glancing at their partner who was halfway down the street. "Erm. Bye."

Lillie watched them go with curiosity, sensing there might've been something more to their relationship, but not wanting to press.

"Your chocolate, as requested," he said, placing the bag on Lillie's display counter. "Feel free to inspect it."

Lillie opened the bag, immediately hit by the scent of earthy chocolate. There were eight bars and a large paper box of powder. She smiled, satisfied. "Thank you so much. This will be perfect."

"Surprised to see the McTavishes in here," Mr. Calcut said, sliding to the window to peer outside.

"Really?" Lillie asked, breaking a small bit of the chocolate off to taste it. "Why's that?"

"Oh, they're not much for *magical* things, in my experience." He turned to her, a knowing smirk on his lips. "Jan McTavish is *quite* fond of iron."

"They...are?" Lillie lowered the bag. Iron was the antithesis to magic, and magical creatures could ingest it to dampen or even erase their powers. Lillie had even taken a few doses when the queen's soldiers had been in town, to be on the safe side.

"Mm." He nodded. "Well, I can't be sure if they're still fond of it. Since we've had a new blacksmith come to town, I haven't been asked to procure any iron powder."

"Iron powder?" Lillie asked. That was even more suspicious. No reason for that other than to hide magic.

Again, he dipped his head. "But as I said, it's been about a year since I've gotten it for them. If that will be all, I'll take my payment."

Lillie crossed the kitchen to fetch the gold and added an extra silver. "Thank you for your expediency. There's a trio of young ladies who are dying for more chocolate chip cookies."

"I'll be sure to stop in next week," he said with a bow. "Until next time…"

Chapter Thirteen

Lillie wasn't one to judge people for doing whatever they needed to avoid arrest, but if Mr. Calcut was right, the McTavishes were definitely hiding something. Iron powder didn't have any use—at least, to Lillie's knowledge—other than to dampen magic.

So was Jan magical?

It seemed hypocritical, then, that they'd send a letter to the Kovens decrying them for having it, calling Nikola a cheater. Lillie could see a scenario where Jan *had* magic but was doing their best to dampen the effects. Perhaps to keep themself safe from the queen, but maybe they disliked that part of themself and didn't want anyone else to have it, either.

Lillie wasn't quite ready to confront Jan McTavish until she had more information, so the next morning, she rose and whipped up strawberry muffins (a variation on the cupcakes, with a touch less sugar), then made vanilla cupcakes with vanilla buttercream icing, and two dozen chocolate chip cookies. She hadn't seen those young women again, but Lillie had another destination in mind for the cookies.

Gilda Climber was the only other person from Pigsend who'd taken Mr. Abora up on his invitation. Lillie hadn't yet visited with the blacksmith, though Earl and Etheldra had popped in when they were helping Lillie get ready. Gilda had even donated the beautiful tables and chairs in Lillie's shop, telling Earl the person who'd bought them hadn't wanted them.

Lillie realized with a start that person was *probably* Julian Globe.

"Well, I hope he doesn't come down here, then," she muttered. "Might accuse me of theft."

Not that he'd recognize them now. Earl had painted them with several coats to keep the iron's anti-magic properties somewhat contained.

Iron or not, she was indebted to Gilda for donating them to the shop, so she boxed up an assortment of goodies to take her. Of course, Lillie first wanted to know if she was providing iron powder to the McTavishes. But Lillie also wanted to confirm the blacksmith didn't know about Lillie's past. Gilda had left for Silverkeep about two months after Lillie had arrived in Pisgend, so Lillie didn't *think* the blacksmith knew anything about her. But it was also possible she knew more than she let on. After all, her former master Gore had been able to hide his supernatural hearing ability with his proximity to iron. Gilda could've been hiding some unknown powers, too.

The Silverkeep Forge was off the town square, an open building that radiated heat even out to the street. Lillie stepped under the awning, looking around the room filled with tools, shovels, iron-rimmed barrels, and boxes of nails sitting on every surface. Lillie kept her distance from all of it, as venturing too close to iron made her head swim.

The blacksmith herself was working in the back, wearing a mask while she hammered a mallet onto a white-hot object. Gilda turned, noticing she had a customer, then dunked the object into a nearby barrel of water, where it sizzled loudly. She opened her mask and gave Lillie a friendly smile.

"Morning! What can I do for you today?"

"Oh, hello," Lillie said, realizing Gilda didn't recognize her. "My name is Lillie Dean. I'm...from Pigsend."

"Right! You're the one who came in with Earl and Etheldra!" Gilda put her mask down and crossed the forge to shake Lillie's hand. The other woman wasn't much taller than Lillie, but she was all muscle. She had brown hair swept back in a braid and a smile that seemed as bright as the white-hot iron she'd dunked in the water. "So sorry. Sometimes when I work in the forge too long, my mind takes a minute to reset. I'm sure you understand, being a baker and all."

"I do," Lillie said.

"What can I do for you?"

"I popped in to bring you a little treat," Lillie said, plopping the box of goodies on the table next to her. "Former Pigsend resident to former Pigsend resident."

"That's very kind of you." Gilda peered into the box. "My, doesn't this look delicious. Reminds me of Etheldra's tea shop. I used to go there for a midmorning snack every day. Get one of Mackey's scones. Once he started making them properly, that is." She picked up the cupcake and took a bite. "You're the one who made him good, right?"

Lillie smiled. "I wouldn't say that. He was already skilled, just needed a bit of guidance. It was my honor to work with him, to be honest. And now, well, he doesn't need my help anymore, that's for sure. He's probably busier than he knows what to do with."

"Hope so," Gilda said, stuffing two cookies into her mouth. "Where's your bakery located, anyway?"

"Down by the wharf," Lillie said. "I think Mr. Abora was trying to stimulate business down there. Though he offered you a spot to the north, didn't he?"

"Didn't have a choice," Gilda said, licking her fingers. "The forge and all the equipment were already here, you know? Suppose it's for the best. Not much down by the wharf, though I do make a fair number of barrels for the merchants. 'Course, they get their burly men to pick 'em up and take 'em down to the ships." She cracked a wry smile. "Not that I'm complaining. I like a man who can pick up heavy things."

Lillie's cheeks turned red as the blacksmith chuckled lewdly. "Well. I'm so happy your business is thriving. Have you had any trouble with the old owner coming back to reclaim their property?"

Gilda shook her head. "I've heard about other people struggling with it, but no. The old blacksmith went off to fight in the war—kingside—and, erm. Let's say he probably shoulda stayed home." She cringed. "In any case, blacksmithing isn't quite as common as seamstressing or probably baking, so I don't think I'll have to worry." She paused. "Why? Did someone come to your shop claiming they owned it? I saw a line out the door at the town hall."

"Not quite," Lillie said. "But... Well, there've been some rumblings about the folks Mr. Abora invited to town. Some people don't appreciate the newcomers. I wanted to make sure you hadn't experienced any of that."

"Nah. I daresay everyone's happy to have a blacksmith at their beck and call. I'm busier than I know how to handle. Asked my sister Valta if she wanted to move here, but my parents said no." She chuckled. "Poor girl's the last one in Pigsend. Her two idiot friends left for Sheepsburg, and I left for Silverkeep. But I told her someone's gotta stay behind and man the farm, and it clearly ain't gonna be me."

"I do hope you'll come down to visit me sometime soon. I don't have tea, but—"

"Yeah, I've been to that Globe Café, but bleh." She made a face. "You should teach that guy how to bake, like you taught Mackey. Nothing I got there is any good. Just glad they have tea, but even that doesn't hold a candle to what Etheldra used to make." She sighed. "I really miss Pigsend sometimes, you know?"

"I do, too. Especially Bev and Allen," Lillie said. "I did have one question for you..." She wasn't sure how to phrase it. "Do you know where I came from before Pigsend?"

Gilda shook her head. "No, can't say that I do. But Gore had me working sunup to sundown at the forge, so I barely got to speak to anyone." She chuckled. "I bet he's really sore that I'm not there. He looked like I'd betrayed him when I told him I was moving. I've sent him a few letters, but I haven't heard back." She looked a little guilty. "I hope he's all right. Not working himself to the bone."

"He was gone for a bit," Lillie said. "Helping to defeat the queen."

"What? *Gore*?" Gilda laughed. "Gore? What in the world would he have to do with *that*?"

Lillie feigned a smile. Gilda really *didn't* have any clue about the secret happenings in Pigsend, which meant she probably didn't know about Lower Pigsend, either. "I'm sure you'll get a letter from him soon. He was getting his bearings back when I left. He'll have *a lot* to tell you."

Gilda let out a breath. "Boy, you said it. Gore? My Gore? Fighting for the king? He never breathed a word of it to me. Mind you, we didn't do much talking, but—"

Lillie could scarcely believe that, with as much as Gilda seemed to want to chat. "I did have one more question for you. Are you familiar with the McTavishes?"

"Oh, yeah, they come in from time to time," she said. "Well, Jan does. Don't see Orxan that often."

"What all do you sell Jan? Any kind of iron powder?"

"Yes, actually." She rubbed the back of her head. "I mean, maybe they've got weak blood or something. No idea why they'd need a bucket full of iron powder once a month."

"And they've been in recently to buy it?" Lillie asked.

"Jan was here yesterday getting more. They don't seem to love me for some reason, not sure why. I have that effect on people. My mom used to say my personality was too big, you know?"

Lillie smiled. "I think your personality is perfect. They do seem rather…skittish, you know?"

"Skittish is the right word. The moment they walked into the shop, they seemed like they couldn't breathe. Like being in my presence was painful to them." She picked up the last cookie and stuffed it in her mouth. "Where did you say your bakery was again? Gonna have to make a special trip."

~

Lillie gave Gilda directions, and the blacksmith promised to come visit soon. Despite her gregarious nature, Lillie really did like Gilda and was happy to have someone from Pigsend so close.

"But oh, to be a fly on the wall when that letter comes from Gore," Lillie muttered.

She bypassed the bakery, which didn't have a single waiting customer, and continued down to the wharf. Jan was getting iron powder from the blacksmith to hide magic, of that Lillie had no doubt. But were they the letter writer, too—and if so, *why*? Was it hatred of all things magic? Jan had seemed awfully eager to leave the bakery and hadn't wanted to eat anything that might've had magic in it.

There was only one way to get at the truth—and that was to ask the fisherfolk themselves. She waved briefly to Ursil and Kristin but continued until she found Orxan alone at their booth, which meant Jan was either out to sea or at their boat. Lillie stood at the back of the dock and gazed out onto the various slips. The Jacob twins were hauling in fish. Lawson and Hipolita were talking on their boat. Nikola's slip was empty. A few other fisherfolk she hadn't met yet were milling around, too.

There. Jan was sitting on their boat, eating a sandwich.

Lillie screwed up her courage and marched over, mentally rehearsing what she was going to say. Would she come out with the accusation? What if she was wrong, and the fisherfolk *wasn't* responsible? Best to keep most of her cards close to the vest until she knew for sure. After all, she could make things much worse for Nikola if she opened her big mouth and blabbed.

"Excuse me," Lillie said, coming to Jan's slip. Luckily, no one else was around so they'd have a semi-private conversation.

Jan spun, giving Lillie a look that seemed a

mixture of surprise and fear. "Oh, it's you. What do you want? I don't want any of your sweets today, baker."

"I have a question for you," Lillie said. "Do you have a problem with me?"

This wasn't what the fisherfolk had been expecting, as they turned all the way around and hopped to their feet. "I'm sorry?"

"I want to know if you have a problem with me. My openly living as a magical creature. My bakery. Any of that."

"N-no?" They looked honestly confused. "Why would you say that?"

"You refused to eat any of my baked goods," Lillie said, folding her arms over her chest.

"Well, yeah, I..." They shifted uncomfortably. "I, erm... Not much for sweets."

"Is that it?" Lillie took a step forward. "Or is it because you're the one sending nasty letters, threatening to expose secrets if I don't leave town?"

The fisherfolk blinked once, twice, then slowly shook their head. "I have...no idea what you're talking about. I've got no quarrel with you. I don't want to eat your magical stuff, that's all." They tilted their head. "But if I were a betting person, I'd put my money on Julian Globe sending that to you."

"Julian Globe has no problem with the Kovens," Lillie said, again, choosing her words carefully. "Who also got a letter."

That earned a reaction. Jan quickly put their sandwich down and hurried off the boat, taking Lillie by the arm and walking away a few steps, even though there was no one around. "What are you talking about? Why would you think I threatened the Kovens?"

"Ursil got a note from someone threatening to…do something if they didn't pack up and leave," Lillie said. "They said Nikola was cheating. You were in my shop the other day, saying you don't like cheaters." She wrested her arm out of the fisherfolk's grasp. "Though I suppose the pot's calling the kettle black, since you've been ingesting iron powder."

"How…" They swallowed. "How did you know that?"

"I'll tell you if you tell me why you wrote the letter."

"I swear to you, on my partner's life, I didn't write any letter—to you or the Kovens." They took a step back. "The Kovens are half the reason Orxan and I get to keep the Fisherfolk Council. It would be devastating if they left."

"Really?" Lillie furrowed her brow.

"Oh, yeah. The rest of these morons can't fish their way out of a paper bag," Jan said, gesturing to the docks behind them. "It's only thanks to Nikola constantly bringing in the fish that Mr. Globe doesn't look too closely into the Fisherfolk Council." They shifted. "Orxan and I…may not be paying exactly the ten percent that's in our agreement with him. But you know, times are tough. And he's already got so much money."

"I see..." Lillie said with a slow nod. "You two haven't gotten any nasty letters lately, have you?"

"Not that I know of," they said. "But... The Kovens can't leave. I forbid it." They swallowed. "You have to figure out who wrote to them and tell them to knock it off. There's no way we can keep up with the quotas without them."

"Working on it," Lillie said. "To be honest, Ursil's the one who thought it was someone from the wharf who'd sent it. Someone with anti-magic sentiments."

Jan snorted. "So you thought it was me?"

"You've had a very anti-magic attitude about you," Lillie said. "You've been ingesting iron powder, and you refused to eat anything from my bakery—and don't say it's because you don't like sweets." Before the fisherfolk could reply, she added, "Because you looked like they were poisonous."

"I didn't want to eat anything from your shop because I wasn't sure what it would do to me," they said. "And I ingest the powder because...well, I'm part fairy."

Chapter Fourteen

That was certainly not what Lillie had been expecting to hear. "Part...what?"

"Fairy." They sighed. "My dad was a fairy. Pink wings, fairy dust, the whole thing. Met my mom—don't ask me how they made me, but here I am." They gestured to the ocean. "But my dad, being a fairy, didn't stick around long. So we started a new life here. I started taking iron powder to dull the effects of my dad's magic when I was a teenager."

"I...see..." Lillie said, still not quite able to envision the fisherfolk as anything other than human. "So I was right, kinda. You don't want to have magic."

"Fairy magic is....well, mixed with human blood, it's not that much fun," they said. "I started sprouting wings and leaving behind a trail of dust—which, at my size, was a *lot* of dust, you know?"

Lillie could see that.

"Then the queen came to power, and it was only thanks to the powder that I escaped arrest. If I'd known what she was doing, I'd have given it to every fisherfolk in the wharf." They sighed. "Then it was Orxan and me, having to fish for the entire town. When all the transplants showed up—starting with the Kovens—Orxan and I realized we could take advantage, you know? It was always a free-for-all in the before times. You had a boat, but you didn't always have a slip. We put some rules in place."

"Rules that benefited you," Lillie said, eyeing them.

"Mr. Globe doesn't look too closely as long as we keep the wharf market full of fish," they said, pointing to the large ships on the other side of the dock. "But if we stopped bringing in so many, he might decide it's more lucrative to get rid of the fisherfolk altogether and bring in another of these big ships. Orxan and I keep him happy to the benefit of everyone. That includes making sure Nikola Koven always keeps her slip."

Lillie could certainly see how they thought they

were being altruistic, but there was still a dash of self-serving. But it seemed this fisherfolk was too busy hiding their own identity to care about Nikola. "Don't suppose you've heard any rumors about where I'm from, have you?"

They shook their head. "Why?"

"Because my letter threatened to expose a secret from my past," Lillie said.

"I can't say anyone knows where you came from," Jan said. "Roudie was talking about how you were in a big fight with Benetta, but he didn't know specifics. Said you'd tried to give her some bad pastries but decided against it."

Lillie winced, wishing the dockworker hadn't been sharing *that* bit of information.

"I swear, I don't know anything about any secrets you have," Jan said. "Nor do I know of anyone else who does."

"Then I'm at a dead end," Lillie said with a sigh. "The Kovens and I are both being targeted, and I haven't a clue who would do it or why. I went to the library to see if maybe the person who owned the building before we moved in was back, but they haven't shown up yet." She paused. "Does the name Moussison ring any bells?"

"No, that's..." They frowned. "That's not who owned the shop before you."

"That's what the archive says," Lillie said. Perhaps the librarian had pulled the wrong year.

"Reynard Moussison was the owner before the war."

"No idea who that was. But the shop was owned by a kappa boat maker named Wani." They gestured to the dinghy bobbing in the slip. "He made my boat, too. He was arrested. I watched them haul him away." They swallowed. "Not that iron would've hidden that turtle shell, but he's one of the ones I regret not helping."

"That's odd," Lillie said. She didn't want to go back up to the archive, but it might be worth a double check.

"You aren't…gonna tell anyone about this little chat, are you? Least of all Orxan." They shook their head. "No clue what he'd say if he found out his partner was really…"

"I'm sure he'd be fine with it," Lillie said softly. "You're still you, no matter if you have magic or not."

"I can't take that chance," they said. "In any case, forgive me if I decline your delicious cupcakes and muffins."

"Understandable," Lillie said. "But if you're worried my pastries will trigger something, I can make sure to remove all magic in anything I serve you. It really isn't a hardship for me. But if you really hate sweets—"

Jan smiled—the first one Lillie had ever seen on the fisherfolk. "I actually love lemon bread."

"Then as soon as I find lemons, I'll make some

for you," she said with a grin. "And don't worry, your secret is safe with me. As long as you let the Kovens live in peace."

Lillie returned to the bakery, feeling both relieved and confused, and dreading the walk back to the archive. She doubted Sexton would be any kinder to her, though she'd be sure to leave the cupcakes behind this time.

Still, that task would be better left to tomorrow. She'd already spent most of the day away from the bakery—not that she had a line of customers, but Ursil had been right about her needing to stick around. What she wouldn't give for a bakery assistant—though she couldn't even afford to pay herself yet.

Everything was already clean and tidy, so Lillie rearranged the pastries in the window display and case. The cookies she put in the front, hoping to signal to that trio of girls who'd been by before that there were more in stock. Then she wiped the windows and the glass of the case, even though they were already clean.

She sat on her stool in the front of the shop and sighed. She supposed she should've expected things to be slow, but she'd been so used to her busy shop in Lower Pigsend and the bakery in Pigsend, she hadn't even considered it. Of course, the fact that no one except servants seemed to come down this way probably played a big hand in things, too.

Lillie rose from her stool and walked to the window, looking at the empty shops. Eventually, Mr. Abora was going to untangle the mess he'd made for himself, and *presumably* there would be more shopkeepers than shops around the square. Hopefully, that meant Lillie might get a neighbor or two.

She considered for a moment how odd it was that the only people who'd come back were the ones who'd owned property around the town square. But Ursil had said there'd always been a divide in Silverkeep, so perhaps the rich folk had been able to buy their way to safety. It left an uncomfortable feeling in Lillie's stomach. Although the queen was defeated, the damage she'd wrought would be felt for generations.

A mop of green caught Lillie's attention, and the woman from the town hall walked inside excitedly. She approached the display case, her hands clasped, and inhaled.

"This place smells *heavenly*," she said with a sigh.

"I think so, too," Lillie said, rushing around to stand behind the display case. "The pastries taste pretty good, too, if you ask me."

"I've had dreams about that cupcake," she said, walking up to the case and peering inside. "I'm Wineke, by the way. Wineke Sloos. My partner and I... Well, we *used* to own an apothecary shop north of town. Apparently, it's now owned by Mr. Globe." She made a face. "But hopefully, we'll get it back soon."

"Lovely to meet you," Lillie said, also introducing herself. "What are you craving today?"

"Gosh, all of it?" She chuckled. "It's been such a stressful few days since we left Lower Silverkeep. One day, we're at our shop, making potions and minding our business. The next, someone comes running into town swearing up and down the queen's been defeated, and we can come out of hiding."

"I had a similar experience," Lillie said.

"Do you think…" She peered at Lillie over the case. "Do you think it's true?"

"I do. Else I wouldn't be here, you know?" Lillie shrugged.

"Right, you are being rather…open with your magic, aren't you?" She shivered then looked into the case. "We didn't have pobyds down in Lower Silverkeep."

"Were you protected by anything?" Lillie asked. "I spent a few years under the protection of a wizard. He cast a charm to keep us safe."

She shook her head. "A local mage made an air bubble in a cave not too far from here. You could only get there by going underwater, you know? I don't think the queen's people could do that. Since they hated magic and all."

"Smart."

"Oh, my. I don't know what to choose." She straightened. "What do you think? What's the best thing you've made?"

"I'd start with the cookies, for sure," Lillie said. "Chocolate always lowers my stress level."

Wineke didn't take much convincing, and soon she was savoring one of the half dozen chocolate chip cookies.

"How's it going up at the town hall?" Lillie asked. "Any progress?"

"None," Wineke said with a sigh. "Mr. Abora says he's working on it, whatever that means. But there are clearly plenty of vacancies down here. The people who moved here should clear out and let us get our place back." She sighed. "Though I'm sure wresting control from Mr. Globe is going to be a feat."

"What's his story?" Lillie asked. "Before the queen, I mean."

"He was a regular merchant, like the rest of them," Wineke said. "Only difference is that he didn't have any magic. That used to put him at a disadvantage, but after the queen came through…" She pursed her lips. "It's not fair that he could buy up everything. Not fair that he's put his name on everything. I'm not even sure that's legal, you know?"

"I know you lived up at the town square, but do

you know anything about who lived here before I did?" Lillie asked. "I checked the library and the archivist—"

"He's awful, isn't he?" She made a face. "Another transplant."

"Yes, he's not very nice," Lillie said. "But he said the previous owner was a Reynard Moussison. But I was chatting with someone at the wharf today, and they said the previous owner was a kappa named Wani."

Wineke shrugged. "No clue. I didn't spend much time down here. There was another apothecary on this side of town, if memory served. We had our clients, they had theirs." She shifted. "I'm honestly not sure how many of our clients survived. I didn't see too many folks I recognized at the town hall."

"It's interesting that most of the people who've returned lived up north," Lillie said. "And that no one down here seems to be back to reclaim their property."

The apothecary shifted uncomfortably. "Yes, well. Some people were lucky. We all had to do what was necessary to save our necks, you know? I'm sure the same could be said for you, too."

When the soldiers had come to do their inspections, Lillie had read the tea leaves and followed a group of magical folks to Lower Pigsend from Sheepsburg. At the time, she hadn't thought about how lucky she'd been to have even *heard* about it, but thinking about it now, she really had been truly fortunate.

"Yes, I suppose so." She brightened, not wanting her brand-new customer to feel like she was being judged. "Well, you're back now. And hopefully soon, everyone will have a place to lay their heads. In the meantime, why don't you take a pastry or two back with you?"

At sundown, Lillie locked the bakery for the day. Wineke promised to be back, bringing her partner next time, and Lillie would hopefully see Gilda in the next few days for a morning scone. Business was finally starting to pick up, but she was no closer to figuring out who was behind these letters, or what their goals were. Other than Benetta, who could've been lying about who she'd told, but probably wasn't, no one else knew her secret. Not only that, there weren't many people who knew the Kovens', either.

She thought back to a similar situation in Pigsend, when Gore, Gilda's old boss, had been revealed to be a kitsus, a magical creature with enhanced hearing. She chuckled to herself as she tidied the front room, wondering if she should walk the town whispering and seeing if someone noticed.

Wineke had requested raspberry pastries, and Lillie made a mental note to make some lemon bread for Jan. Luckily, she had plenty of flour and sugar, and with Kristin's morning deliveries and the wharf market down the street, she wouldn't be wanting for fruits to turn into sweet fillings.

With a yawn, Lillie glanced at the bread starter sitting in a jar. She'd dutifully fed it, as per Bev's instructions had said, but she hadn't made bread in a few days.

"Really should think about making that in the morning," Lillie vowed to herself.

With that, she headed for the door, realizing too late that she didn't have *anything* for dinner. A scone would have to do, but it wouldn't be that filling. When she reached the landing of her apartment, though, she found a paper-wrapped object sitting in front of her door. Curious, and worried for a moment it was another threat, she carefully opened the wrapping to reveal a filet of fish that had been smoked and seasoned. Lillie inhaled, her mouth watering, and said a silent *thank you* to her lovely neighbors next door as she carried it into her apartment.

She took a bite, unable to believe the absolute explosion of flavors. Spice and heat and earthy herbs and even lemon filled her mouth as she worked her way through the flaky white flesh. She knew sweets inside and out, but she'd have to ask Nikola about this recipe for sure.

After the delicious dinner, Lillie made a pot with

the last of Etheldra's tea and settled in with her scone, thinking about the day. When she gathered the courage to write to her friends back in Pigsend, she'd have to ask Etheldra to send more, and include an extra satchel or two for Gilda. But once again, Lillie found she couldn't pick up the quill sitting at the ready. Not until she—

"Excuse me."

Lillie let out a yelp, spinning around in the direction of the voice. She held her breath, scanning the one-room apartment. No one was there. "H-hello?"

"Yes. Down here."

She once again looked around the room, finding no one.

"Ahem. *Down* here."

She tilted her head lower, lower, lower until she found the source of the voice. It was a mouse, no bigger than a teacup, standing on his hind legs wearing a stylish three-piece suit and carrying a small bag. His whiskers twitched as she approached slowly.

"Can I...help you?" Lillie said, kneeling to his level. She'd seen magical mice in Lower Pigsend, of course, but was surprised to see one in her apartment.

"My name is Reynard Moussison," he said. "And I'm here to collect the rent."

Chapter Fifteen

"*You're* Mr. Mous…" *Mouse*-ison.

"Call me Rey," he said, putting down his bag and walking forward to shake her hand—or rather, to gently grasp her pinky with both his little claws. He carried himself like a mouse with purpose, as if he were used to speaking with and demanding rents from creatures much larger than himself. "And you are—?"

"Lillie Dean," she said.

"How long have you lived in my property, Miss Dean?"

"About a month."

"You've certainly spruced up the place. It looks wonderful," he said, very matter-of-factly. "Surely, Nikola Koven told you about me."

"She...didn't," Lillie said. "Neither did Ursil."

"Well, that's because *Mr.* Koven fainted the first time we spoke," Rey said with a chuckle. "I deal primarily with *Ms.* Koven. Love that woman. Always has the best fish."

Lillie wasn't quite sure what to say. When she'd moved in, Mr. Abora had said that her rent had been waived for the first month while she got her feet under her, but after that, she'd be paying ten gold coins to Mr. Globe. "To be honest, I wasn't aware that you were the owner. I checked the town records, and the librarian said you'd abandoned it—"

He bristled. "Abandoned it! Falsehoods and lies! I've been living in these walls since I could barely open my eyes as a child."

"You...have?" Lillie frowned. "So you didn't have to hide from the queen?"

"I mean, I didn't exactly make my presence *known* to her soldiers," he said. "But being the size I am, it's easy to keep out of sight. That doesn't mean I haven't been here, though." He put his tiny hands on his hips. "Who do you think owns this place?"

"Mr. Globe?" Lillie said.

"That cad!" Rey practically spat. "Too big for his britches, if you ask me. Weeeell, let me tell you this,

Miss Dean, if you look at the town records, you will find *my* name on them! And if that Sexton Cliffton fellow has overwritten my name with Mr. Globe's, we are going to have to have some *words*, let me tell you!"

Lillie could only imagine the fastidious librarian coming face-to-face with a mouse, even one so nicely dressed. He was panting now, and seemed quite hot under the collar, and Lillie could picture him marching up to the library and causing a fuss.

Lillie held up her hand in surrender. "I think we should back up. I'll tell you what I know, and you can tell me what you know. Then perhaps we can figure out what's going on."

Rey agreed, and Lillie told him about Mr. Abora soliciting her to move, about him granting her the lease to the downstairs shop and upstairs apartment, and how she'd been here for almost a whole month.

"Which begs the question," Lillie said gently. "Where've you been these past few weeks if not hiding?"

He chuckled. "I was out west visiting my sisters. They've had another litter, so I thought it was a good excuse to see family." He puffed up his chest. "I suppose the timing was coincidental, but I do own this building, including the apartments and bakery. I'm very surprised Nikola didn't tell you."

"More surprised Mr. Abora told me Mr. Globe was the landlord," Lillie said, adding that to the list of things she was going to ask him about—whenever she could get ahold of him. "How long have you owned this building?"

"It's been in my family for generations," he said. "I'm technically Reynard Moussison the eighth, if you can believe it. My many-times great-grandfather owned all kinds of property around town, but unfortunately, his descendants weren't quite so good at navigating the world of the larger folk, so our property ownership dwindled. Now, I own this building, and have since my father retired two years ago."

"Has anyone else ever claimed ownership?"

"Not to my knowledge," he said. "Before the war, a pair of selkies who lived in the Kovens' place, and a kappa lived here and ran the shop."

"Wani, right?" Lillie said.

He nodded. "Lovely fellow. We had lots of conversations on the right type of wood and varnish to use." He sighed forlornly. "But they were all arrested."

"Any chance they'd want to come back?" Lillie asked. "Reclaim their spots?"

He shook his head. "The Mouse Whisper Network is quite vast, and last year, I was able to confirm that they'd been…" He sighed and wiped away a tear. "It was like I lost Wani twice when I heard the news."

Lillie nodded. "I'm so sorry. I suppose I was

fortunate that my parents died in a spate of dragon pox before the war. So many people don't know what became of their loved ones." She thought of Benetta and hoped her sister had made a reappearance.

"Enough about that," he said, shaking himself. "You're here now, and it's clear you're going to stay for a long time. The shop has never looked so beautiful! Imagine my surprise coming home to the incredible scents of sugar and chocolate."

So you're not sending letters to get us to vacate. That was a good thing, in any case. "You keep mentioning your home," Lillie said. "Where is it, exactly?"

"Between the walls." He pointed to the small hole Lillie hadn't noticed before. "Obviously, I don't take up much space. Happy to let the property to folks who can use it and collect the rents, as any good landlord does."

"And what is the rent?" Lillie asked. She didn't particularly want to take this nice mouse to Mr. Abora, but she also couldn't afford to pay hundreds of gold coins to a small mouse *and* Mr. Globe. Where would Rey put it anyway? And what would he use it for? The mice back in Lower Pigsend had their own currency, so Lillie had heard. They kept to themselves and rarely interacted with the larger folks.

Rey's whiskers twitched. "Well, you've got quite

the repertoire of baked goods, don't you? I'd like to have a little something set aside for me every day."

Lillie opened and closed her mouth. "Really? That's it?"

"Nikola pays her rent in smoked fish," he said. "If you haven't tried her recipe yet, you absolutely should. But I find that's a fair bargain."

Lillie would *very* much like to talk with Nikola about this mouse, his rents, and what in the world was going on with it. Perhaps the fisherfolk was merely humoring the mouse, giving him fish to keep him from chewing holes in her socks, while paying the actual rent to Mr. Globe. But Lillie could spare a cookie or muffin for her nice little mouse landlord, at least until everything was sorted.

"I think that'll be fine," Lillie said. "I'm up at four to bake. Feel free to pop in at any time to get your payment." She cleared her throat, looking at the small door near her bed. "Are you…planning on coming to visit the apartment often?"

"Not at all," he said, puffing out his chest as he surveyed the room. "As long as you keep the apartment clean and well-kept, I don't see a reason to come in at all, unless invited, of course." He spotted the purple-wool quilt on the bed. "Ah, it looks like you have a tanddaes-owning friend? Been a while since I've seen one of those."

"I did, back where I came from," Lillie said.

"Might I…have a bit of that?" Again, his

whiskers twitched, but this time, Lillie read the excitement. "I do love the feel of it. Nothing keeps the chill out in the winter better or keeps me cool in the summer."

"That was made for me by a dear friend," Lillie said, unable to fathom taking scissors to Merv's quilt. "But...next time I write him a letter, I'll see if he can't send a small swatch. There are loads of tanddaes down in Lower Pigsend."

"Ah, I heard about that place!" he said. "My sister said some of my cousins emerged from there. Spent six years underground hiding out from Her Majesty."

"Maybe I knew them," Lillie said, though she rather hoped she didn't. Would Rey's opinion change if he knew she was nearly responsible for his cousins' endangerment? Maybe try to evict her? "Well, in any case, I do have to be getting to bed. Early morning for us bakers. If there's anything else I can do for you—"

"No. I think we're going to get on quite well." He extended one of his small, delicate arms and Lillie touched her pinky to it. "Pleasure doing business with you, Ms. Dean."

"Call me Lillie."

~

Lillie would have to wait to pick Nikola's brain—and Mr. Abora's—about the curiosity that was Reynard Moussison, but at least she could mark off the owner of the building *and* the former tenants as possible letter-writers. Of course, that didn't bring her closer to the answers she was looking for. Someone out there wanted her and the Kovens to leave, and since they didn't seem to be after their property, all signs pointed to the culprit wanting two magical creatures who were invited to town by Mr. Abora gone.

Yet again, she had too many unsold pastries and was starting to stretch the limits of her freshening spell. Other than Wineke the day before, she hadn't sold anything. So although it went against her very nature, Lillie didn't bake anything new, opting to save her ingredients.

Ursil arrived right at ten, and luckily Rey was nowhere to be found. She greeted him, offering a scone, which he took with a grimace but didn't eat.

"Have you made any headway on those letters yet?" he asked. "I saw you down with the McTavishes yesterday. Did they confess to it?"

"Not quite," Lillie said. "But you can rest assured that the McTavishes very much like having you and Nikola around. I think we can safely mark them off the list."

"Huh." He picked off a piece. "Well, that's disappointing. Any of the other fisherfolk seem like they're behind it?"

Lillie shook her head. "I also don't think it's someone who wants us to move, either. I, erm, have it on good authority that the prior tenants aren't coming back. And the owner—"

"Mr. Globe."

"Yes, Mr. Globe," Lillie said. "I think there's some other piece of this puzzle I'm missing, unfortunately. And until someone gets another letter, I think I'm at a standstill." She tilted her head. "It's been a few days since we've gotten ours. Maybe whoever sent them has decided to leave us alone?"

Lillie wasn't optimistic, but that was all she had to offer Ursil. The fishmonger headed to the market, promising to keep his ears open for anything else, and Lillie wasn't too far behind him. She needed to clear her head and replenish her produce.

She approached produce farmer Ewing's booth, which was filled to the brim with plump strawberries, vibrant blueberries, and fuzzy peaches that smelled delicious, as well as rhubarb, cherries, and—excitingly—a few lemons.

"I know someone who's going to be *very* happy about this," Lillie said with a grin. "Between you and Kristin, you're going to be my dearest friends."

He put his hearing aid to his ear. "What was that?"

"Erm, never mind," Lillie said, paying him. "Thank you!"

She turned to head home, but spotted Nikola's dinghy coming back to the docks and headed over to the fisherfolk part of the market. Ursil hadn't arrived yet, but it was still early in the day.

She waved hello to the fisherfolk who'd come by the shop the day before, watching their expressions for anything that looked like malice. But everyone looked happy and jovial today—but they had a nice haul of fish, so perhaps that was the reason for it.

Nikola was repairing her nets with a needle and rope. She looked up as Lillie approached but didn't stop her mending. "Good morning," she said. "What can I do for you?"

"Well, first, I wanted to thank you for your generous gift yesterday," Lillie said. "It really couldn't have come at a better time."

"You've certainly been keeping Ursil fed," Nikola said, moving the net along to work on another hole. "He's so happy. Which makes me happy. And I haven't seen you eat anything substantial lately. Important to keep your strength up, you know?"

Lillie smiled. "Agreed. My mind's been elsewhere." She cleared her throat. "Do you have a favorite sweet? I'd love to make something for you."

"I'm a simple woman," she said. "I like bread, fish, and cheese."

"Then how about I make you a loaf of bread?" Lillie beamed. "I have a lovely recipe with rosemary."

"If you insist, but please don't make any on my

account." She returned to the net.

Lillie cleared her throat, deciding to come out with it. "Well, I believe I got a visit from our mutual landlord yesterday."

She stopped mending and looked up, surprised. "*Mr. Globe* came down to your shop?"

"Not *that* landlord," Lillie said with a nervous grin.

"Ah." She laughed. "I'm sorry. I should've warned you."

"So he's...really the landlord?" Lillie said. "But you pay rent to Mr. Globe?"

"I pay rent to both, but only one wants to be paid in gold," she said with a chuckle. "When Ursil and I moved in, Mr. Abora told us Mr. Globe was the landlord, and the rent was two gold coins a month. So, the first evening, imagine my surprise when Rey's father poked his head out and asked what we were doing there. His price wasn't too much of a hardship, and I didn't think it pertinent to tell anyone that a magical mouse owned our building—for obvious reasons."

"Yes, but..." Lillie chewed her lip. "I mean, I feel... Well, it doesn't seem right. Rey doesn't want much, but if he's the actual landlord, then it doesn't seem right that you've *also* been paying Mr. Globe."

"I wouldn't think of it as paying rent to Rey," Nikola said with a smile. "I'd think of it as coexisting with a very friendly, very hungry little caretaker who is kind enough to ask all the bugs to clear off while not expecting much in return. He's quite the conversationalist, and knowledgeable about a lot of things. I think being an eighth-generation landowner means he's never had to work for a living, so he threw himself into all kinds of studies. You've never met anyone who knows more about the breeding habits of elves." Nikola picked up the net again. "Though you know, Rey's a big fan of bread, too. So maybe save a slice or two for him."

"I'll do that," Lillie said. She couldn't help feeling someone was getting the short end of the stick. "I think I might go talk with Mr. Abora about all this, if you don't mind. Rey could own the property—he certainly seems to think so. And if that's the case, you shouldn't be paying anything to Mr. Globe."

Nikola put down her net, giving Lillie a serious look. "If you want to rock the boat, do so with your own name. Don't bring us into it."

"I don't think it's rocking—"

"Mr. Globe owns this entire town," Nikola said. "He owns the docks, the slips, the apartment, probably the street we walk on. He might even own the air. No one says a word against him—at least, if they want to keep their home." She inspected the net again. "You spent a lot of time and effort getting your bakery cleaned and ready for customers. I'd hate to see you lose it because you baited the shark."

Lillie pursed her lips. "But if Mr. Globe isn't the owner—"

"And who'll enforce that, hm? Everyone's on his payroll." She met Lillie's gaze again. "Believe me when I say that your time is better spent baking tarts and icing cakes. But if you insist on making the most powerful person in town angry, be sure to leave my and my husband's names out of it."

Chapter Sixteen

Lillie could understand Nikola's hesitation. Mr. Globe did seem to control the town hall, even with all the rowdy transplants. He was already getting pressure from all the folks who'd come back, and Lillie adding her voice to the mix might not go over so well. But if he wasn't truly the owner of the building, then he shouldn't be taking gold from the Kovens—that was an indisputable fact. Whether or not Nikola wanted to rock the boat, the amount of money she'd unnecessarily paid to Mr. Globe over the years... It was almost robbery.

"Mr. Globe's not sending us letters, is he?" Lillie

muttered to herself as she left the market. She doubted the powerful merchant would stoop that low. He'd probably send an eviction note.

A steady stream of people passed Lillie as they headed to the wharf market. She smiled at them, searching their faces for a familiar one. She was still holding out hope those three girls who'd come a few days before would return, though she didn't have any chocolate chips left to serve them. Nor had she seen the Jacob twins in a few days, or any of the other fisherfolk. She was hopeful Wineke would tell the other newly-returned to come down for a sweet or three. It was a bit of a walk, but Lillie thought it was well worth it.

She sighed as she approached the bakery. Once again, no one was waiting, and the pastries in the window were looking puny. Throwing them away would truly be a waste of good sugar and butter. She hummed to herself, propping open the front door to entice someone to come in. But when she walked into the kitchen, she stopped short.

"Good morning!" Rey, dressed in another fine three-piece suit, was sitting on her kitchen table, having taken one of her measuring cups and turned it upside-down, then placed a small tablecloth over it and was enjoying what appeared to be small pieces of a chocolate chip scone. The rest of said scone—about three-quarters remained—was off to the side.

"I hope you don't mind," he said, wiping

crumbs off his face. "I helped myself to my daily sweet. It was too tempting to wait for you to come back."

"That's...quite all right," Lillie said, tossing the rest of the scone into the bin. They had agreed to it, after all, but it was still a bit of a shock to see a finely dressed mouse helping himself to her sellable goods. "I'll be sure to leave something on a plate for you next time." And make something mouse-sized, so she didn't waste anything.

She went for her apron, but noticed two bags on the table, and what appeared to be a box of cocoa powder. Lillie opened the bag and found eight bars of chocolate.

"Mr. Calcut came by?"

"Lovely man. We go way back," Rey said. "He used to bring Wani lacquer for his woodworking, and we'd often chat about the merits of willow bark versus riven flow for pain management. He told me he'd struck a deal with you—eight bars of chocolate and a pound of cocoa powder for a gold coin. That seems quite a good deal, in my opinion."

"I negotiated it myself," Lillie said, a smile growing on her face. "Thank you, Rey. I appreciate you catching him for me."

He wiped his mouth with a tiny napkin then folded it and placed it on the makeshift table. "Really, Lillie. In my opinion, you leave your bakery far too often. People are walking up and down this street all day, and your door is closed. How are you supposed to make a profit if you're never here to sell to them?"

"Well, I don't know if you've heard, but people aren't coming to my bakery, even when it's open," Lillie said.

"Nonsense, you had a stream of visitors the other day! Fisherfolk of all stripes came in."

Lillie turned to him. "How long have you been spying on me?"

Rey cleared his throat, folding the tablecloth and turning the measuring cup back over. "I wouldn't call it *spying*. I wanted to get the measure of you before I introduced myself. Can't be too careful with strangers, you know."

Lillie gave him a sideways look.

"*All* I'm saying is I'm not sure what keeps pulling you out of the bakery, but if you want your business to thrive, you have to be here to run it," he said.

"You're right," Lillie said, looking at the unsold confections on the table. "Unfortunately, there's something else demanding my attention. And until that's resolved, I'm going to have to be in two places at once."

"Unless..." He scampered forward and puffed out his chest. "Well, I think the solution is simple, isn't it?"

"What do you mean?"

"You should hire me."

"Hire...you?" Lillie blinked. Here she thought she was getting a lecture, not a job application. "For...?"

"Well, to run the bakery when you're not here!" he squeaked. "I'm quite good with money, you know. And I can help sell your wares when other business takes you away from the important work."

"I'm not sure you're..." She didn't want to mention his size wasn't quite conducive to stirring large bowls of batter. "Won't people be..." Nor did she want to have to say that folks who weren't used to seeing magical mice about might *really* not want to patronize the bakery if they saw him here. "I don't know if..."

"How about this, then: why don't you teach me how to bake?" he said. "It's always been interesting to me, and I've never had anyone who could teach me. And that way, I can expand your customer base to the smaller clientele."

"Smaller... There are more of you?"

"Well, they aren't fortunate enough to be landlords, like me," he said. "But they live in the walls and the alleys. I'm sure more of them will be coming back, now that the queen's been defeated. There'll be a need for mouse-sized confections and baked goods." His whiskers twitched. "Nikola tells me you bake bread, too. If you can teach me how to bake it... That would be well-received by the folks around town."

"I don't suppose it would hurt," Lillie said as she emptied her basket. "I was going to make more strawberry cupcakes. It might be a little late to start the bread, but I could help it along—"

"What do you mean?"

"I mean with magic," Lillie said, pulling the dough jar toward her. She poured some of it into a bowl then looked at Rey. "Erm, you might need to bring your own equipment. I don't have anything that's…well, sized for you."

"I can manage," he said, walking over to one of the large bowls Lillie had stacked on the table. "I'm used to living in a world that's much bigger than I am."

Lillie still wasn't sure how she felt about having a furry creature so near to her confections, but he seemed fastidious enough, and the suit might keep most of it contained. "Right. So first, we need to hull these strawberries." She picked up a knife, one that was longer than Rey was tall. "I don't know if you can help me with this."

"Oh, of course I can. Don't be silly," he said, walking over to the basket and picking up a strawberry. He swayed a bit under the weight but carried it over with some effort and placed it in front of her. "One!"

Lillie dragged the basket closer but reached into her drawer to find another paring knife. It was still as large as Rey, but at least she wouldn't be slowed down by him. "How about you help me hull?"

Unsurprisingly, the mouse did little to expedite the process (having managed to remove one stem by the time Lillie finished the entire basket), but he was nice company. He told Lillie all about growing up in Silverkeep as the eldest of twenty children, and how he was fortunate enough to inherit the family land when his father decided to retire.

"But not before he sent me off to school. I learned as much as I could, spending all day in every class I could find a hole in."

Lillie started as she tipped the bowl of hulled strawberries into the pot. *Find a hole.* "Were you actually enrolled or…?"

"Seeing as Her Majesty didn't like the idea of talking mice, no. But I took the classes all the same. Did all the assignments, read all the books, wrote the essays. Some of the professors had so many students they didn't notice an errant paper in the mix, so I even got a few graded. I'm quite proud of my degree, and now that the queen's gone, I might return to Sheepsburg to officially get it." He bristled. "I mean, not sure how I can prove that I attended classes, but…"

"What does a mouse need with a degree?" Lillie asked while she mashed the strawberries in the pot.

"I'll have you know that there are *lots* of jobs that require degrees," he said with an indignant snort.

"Does landlording?"

"Well, no, but…" He cleared his throat as he walked over to inspect what she was doing. "So we went through the trouble of chopping the tops off so neatly only for you to mash them?"

"You've got to boil the strawberries down," Lillie said, showing him the pot. "First, you mash them to get the juices out. Maybe add a little water to get it going. Once that's done, you put it on low heat until it's reduced in volume by about half. Then you let it cool while you assemble the rest of the cupcakes."

"What does boiling it do?" Rey asked, his nose tipping over the side of the pot. "Oh, that does smell delicious already!"

"Enhances the flavor," Lillie said. "Gives it a little bit of color too, but if I really want them pink, I encourage the berry juice to be bright. I want people to know they're eating a strawberry cupcake."

She put the pot on the stove and stoked the fires so they'd heat the mixture, but not burn. Then she leaned over the pot and whispered, "Keep moving. Don't scald."

The strawberry mixture obeyed, swirling around as if mixed by an invisible spoon.

Rey, still observing from the kitchen table, put his hands on his hips. "Now what are you telling it to do?"

"Suggesting that it stir itself," Lillie said. "That's my magic. I can add intentions to the things I bake, too. Usually, I remind them to taste delicious or not to burn in the oven."

"Do you always have to talk with the food?" Rey asked.

"Not always, but talking to it helps get the point across," Lillie said, turning to the rest of the items on her list to bake. With her chocolate replenished, she could make some more chocolate chip cookies, in case those girls came back—or anyone else came by. "Thank you again for meeting with Mr. Calcut."

"Of course, of course." Rey scampered over to the other side of the table as Lillie opened one of the jugs of milk to pour into another bowl. "What are we making now?"

"Butter for cookies," Lillie said, whispering to the milk to stir and separate. Then, thinking about it, she added more milk to the bowl. "And for the buttercream icing."

"You certainly have quite the useful magical ability," Rey said. "Imagine if you had this power and decided to go into blacksmithing or something like that."

"If I went into blacksmithing, I wouldn't have magic," Lillie said with a chuckle. "Iron repels magic, you know."

"Does it now?"

Lillie nodded. "In fact, back where I came from, the blacksmith *had* magic, but because he was around iron so much, he never tested positive. It wasn't until the magical river overflowed that he even knew he had magic at all."

"Magical river?" He sat on the overturned measuring cup. "What's that?"

Lillie told him all about Pigsend and the curiosities that had occurred in the year she'd lived there, and the ones before she'd arrived, too. It was much faster for her to talk and work, and him to listen rather than try to help. When she finished her story, the cookie dough was made, and she was rolling it into small balls to place on her baking tray.

"Certainly seems like an exciting village," Rey said. "How'd you manage to avoid the queen?"

"I was in a similar place as all the folks who've come out of hiding recently," she said. "I imagine what's happening in Silverkeep is happening all over the place. It can't be easy, this reorienting of the world."

"These kings and queens need to stay on their thrones and leave the rest of us alone," Rey said with a snort. "What does it matter if someone has magic or doesn't? You aren't doing anything other than making delicious things with yours. That's not worth arresting you over—or whatever happened to the rest of the pobyds out there."

"I could see why someone like the queen would

find me dangerous," Lillie admitted quietly. After all, she could *suggest* to baked goods that they unlock all manner of secrets in the person who ate them. That was certainly cause for concern.

"If things were so lovely in Pigsend, what made you want to leave?"

Lillie pressed one of the dough balls onto the baking sheet, flattening it slightly so it would cook more evenly, and thinking her intention that they taste heavenly. "Mr. Abora invited me here. He said the town would grant me this bakery and the apartment above, along with a small stipend to get started."

"Just one problem," Rey said, putting his small hands on his hips. "He wasn't *authorized* to give you anything. This is my property. And I'm quite happy you're here, don't get me wrong. It's such a problem to find good tenants, and you seem to be quite a good one."

"Thank you," Lillie said.

"But I wonder how many other places already had owners that he unilaterally overstepped?" Rey continued. "I mean, it's a good thing Nikola and I have an agreement. Can you imagine her paying *money* to Mr. Globe?"

Lillie turned to him. "I mean...she is paying money to Mr. Globe. Two gold coins every month."

Rey jumped to his feet, his whiskers twitching so fast they blurred. "You can't be serious! Why in the world would she…? He doesn't *own* this building! He has no right to ask her to pay anything at all."

Lillie held up her hands. "I know, I know. I'm also supposed to start paying him at the end of the month. But…I don't think it's right."

"That's because it's *not* right," Rey said with a huff. "I'm the owner. I'm getting my requested rent, and neither of you should be paying that Mr. Globe *anything*." He shook his head. "I think it's high time we meet with him."

"We'll be waiting a while," Lillie said. "There's an entire crowd of magical folks camping out at the town hall right now hoping to meet with Mr. Abora to sort out who owns what. Mr. Globe told him to handle it."

"Then we'll bypass him and go straight to the source." Rey puffed out his chest. "You and I need to meet with Mr. Globe himself. Landlord to landlord, we will sort this out."

Lillie chewed her lip. Rey seemed awfully confident for someone so small, and she could see a world where Mr. Globe picked him up and tossed him out by his tail. Not to mention Nikola's warning.

"I don't know if that's the best course of action," Lillie said. "Nikola was adamant that we not get in the middle of things for her and Ursil. She's happy paying him—"

"Well, *I'm* not," Rey said. "But I won't mention

her involvement. You and I will go. First thing in the morning."

"I don't know if—" She made a face. "Do you think we can get an appointment so quickly? I'm sure he's a busy man."

"Fear not, Lillie. When you've got a mouse by your side, things get done a lot faster than you'd expect." He turned to scamper off the table. "Leave it with me!"

Chapter Seventeen

"We have a meeting with Mr. Globe at eight o'clock."

Rey made this announcement while Kristin unloaded the milk and eggs for the day. The dairy farmer spun, searching for the sound of the voice, until Lillie pointed down.

"What is..." Kristin turned to Lillie. "Who's this? Friend of yours?"

"My name is Reynard Moussison VIII," he said. "I'm Lillie's landlord and new assistant baker."

"Not quite sure about that second part," Lillie muttered. "And we're going to check on the first."

Kristin knelt by Rey, inspecting him. "Kristin Honeygold. Nice to meet you."

"Of Honeygold Farms?"

She nodded.

"I'm terribly sorry, then." He shook his head. "I can only assume you've been acquainted with Penelope Bigears."

"Oh, she's awful," Kristin said. "And she's taken up residence in my barn, so I have to listen to her yammer on and on. No one knows more about scandalous mice shacking up with each other than me, I tell you what."

Lillie smiled. "So you're not surprised to see a talking mouse?"

"Nah. Penelope's the chattiest, but we have a slew of magical mice around the farm," Kristin said, standing back up. "But I've never heard of one being a landlord before. At least, of a building this size. Don't you guys usually stick to the smaller stuff?"

"My many-times great-grandfather was an entrepreneur," he said. "It's in my blood. And we Moussisons have retained this building through many seasons. I'm sure it'll be no problem clearing up the confusion today with Mr. Globe."

"Right." Lillie shook herself. "You said we had an appointment at…eight this morning? How did you manage that?"

"Mice get things done," he said. "I told you I'd handle it, didn't I?"

"Suppose you did," Lillie said. "But erm…" She shared a look with Kristin. "Unfortunately, we're not going to *both* be able to go."

"Well, why not?"

"Someone has to stay and man the bakery, don't they?" Lillie said. "You were telling me yesterday I needed to spend more time here. Mornings are prime time to sell pastries and the like, aren't they?"

"I suppose…" Rey said slowly.

"Might be best if you stayed here and let me handle it," Lillie said.

"Are you sure? I'd hate to let you speak with Mr. Globe alone—"

"You're going to talk with Mr. Globe?" Kristin asked. "Why?"

"We need to sort out the ownership of the bakery," Lillie said.

"We need him to quit demanding gold from my tenants, is what we need," Rey said. "Thieving man!"

"Good luck with that," Kristin said with a look. "From what I hear from the servants, no one's making any headway loosening the folks living at the square. It sounds like all the people who left during the queen's purge aren't getting their property back."

Lillie chewed her lip. "That's awful."

"What are you talking about?" Rey asked.

Lillie briefly told him the situation with the

others around the town square, and he scoffed. "See? What did I tell you? Mr. Globe swept in and stole things that didn't belong to him. Now he's trying to make money off everyone, too. I really should go with you for backup, Lillie. No telling what he'll say or do to you."

"I promise, I'll be fine," Lillie said. "You stay here and keep the shop open for me. We do need to sell some pastries so we can keep buying more ingredients from Kristin."

"Right you are," Kristin said. "Now where's my payment?"

Kristin left with four chocolate chip cookies, and Lillie set to baking until it was time to leave. She whipped up a lemon bread, and told Rey to offer a slice to Jan McTavish, should the fisherfolk make an appearance. But she also made some apple cinnamon muffins, more blueberry scones, and even a few tartlets with fresh raspberries on top. It was close to eight after she plated everything in the display case and front window, so she gave Rey instructions on what to sell and how much each pastry was.

"I'll do my best to clear out the lot before you return," he said, climbing up to sit atop the display case.

Lillie had doubts he'd do anything close to that but appreciated his optimism. She pulled off her apron and hung it on the peg then headed up the hill toward the town square. Mr. Globe's office was, unsurprisingly, in a prime location across from the town hall, and when Lillie opened the door, a sour-faced assistant greeted her.

"Mr. Globe isn't meeting with anyone," she said with an annoyed sigh. "If you have a grievance about your formerly owned property, please take it up with Kemp Abora in the town hall."

"I'm not here about that," Lillie said. "I'm here to—"

"All rent payments are due on the first of the month," she said. "Late payments—"

"I have an appointment," Lillie said. "With Mr. Globe."

The assistant finally looked up, her dark eyes without any hint of friendliness. "No, you don't."

"I was told I did," Lillie said, gesturing to the book sitting by the assistant's hands. "Maybe check the calendar?"

"There's no way you have an appointment, because I didn't *set* an appointment." She flipped open the book, angrily leafing through pages until she reached the current day. "I—"

She stopped suddenly, her gaze falling on the calendar below. Lillie spotted what appeared to be chicken scratch handwriting—perhaps a small mouse holding a large quill?—on the eight o'clock line.

"L-Lillie Dean?"

"That's me," she said. "Is he in?"

"One second."

The girl rose and scrambled back to what Lillie assumed was Mr. Globe's office. Lillie took a seat in one of the nice leather chairs and folded her hands over her legs. A few moments later, the assistant returned, looking pale and scolded.

"G-go on back."

Lillie's palms grew sweaty as she approached the large, glass-inlaid door with the name *Audo Globe, Owner, Globe Merchant Services*. She'd come here expecting to be turned away but now, she was starting to wish she'd rehearsed what she was going to say more.

"Stick to the facts," she whispered to herself, putting her hand on the brass knob. "Stick to the facts."

She opened the door, revealing a spacious office with a large desk, built-in bookshelves filled with thick tomes, and no Audo Globe.

"Over here."

Lillie spun toward the sound of the voice and found the richest man in Silverkeep sitting in one of two armchairs. He had a carafe and an assortment of pastries, presumably from his son's café.

"Please, have a seat. I was about to start my breakfast." He gestured to the open chair across the way. "Coffee?"

"Um, no, thank you," Lillie said, crossing the room stiffly and plopping down.

"Are you sure? It's a Silverkeep delicacy." He poured the dark liquid into one of the two cups sitting on a tray. "I personally selected the farmer and beans from an island down south."

Lillie decided she might want to put her best foot forward. "On second thought, sure. That sounds lovely."

He poured her a cup. "Cream or sugar?"

"Both?" Lillie really wasn't sure what was traditional.

"A pobyd after my own heart." He mixed the two drinks exactly the same and handed her the other cup in a saucer. "Here you are."

"Thank you." Lillie took a sip and found it much more pleasant than the first time she'd tried it. "Oh, now I understand."

"Understand what?" Mr. Globe asked, sitting back and sipping his coffee.

"Nothing," Lillie said, noticing the assortment of pastries. They looked...rough. The muffins seemed too dark and the scones had a black underside. But she held her tongue instead of criticizing. "Thank you so much for agreeing to meet with me."

"It was quite a surprise for Trina," he said, sitting back. "Seeing as she knows I have a strict no-meetings-before-noon policy."

"Oh, well—"

"And the handwriting on her book wasn't hers. Nor was it mine," he continued, watching her like a hawk. "I don't think it was yours, either."

"No, it wasn't." Lillie put down the cup. "Well, you are a busy man, so I suppose we'd better get to it, hm? I'm here because I think there might've been some confusion about the bakery."

"Why do you say that?"

"Well, when I moved in, Mr. Abora assured me that you were the landlord," Lillie said. "And that I was to pay you ten gold coins starting at the first of next month for the bakery and apartment above."

"Yes, that sounds about right."

"Only…the other day," Lillie said, "the…real landlord returned."

"A lot of that going around," he said, sounding as if he were relieved this conversation was over. "Mr. Abora is working to solve that problem. You'll need to make an appointment—"

"I think it's a slightly different situation than the rest of the folks," Lillie said. "You see, Reynard Moussison, the landlord, never left."

Mr. Globe stared at her. "I'm sorry?"

"The landlord. His name is Reynard—Rey, for short. He's actually been living in the building these past six years." Lillie smiled. "So, clearly…"

"I see." Mr. Globe sipped his coffee. "Well, that is cause for confusion, isn't it?"

Lillie nodded and waited for him to say something else, but silence stretched out between them. She looked around, trying to keep from twitching too much, but wished she could read him better. What was he thinking?

"Ms. Dean, I'd like to hire you."

Lillie shook her head. "I'm sorry?"

"I don't think it's any secret that my son Julian's baking skills are lacking," he said with a sigh, picking up one of the muffins. "Look at this. Dry as a bone. You'd think the blueberries would make it edible, but..." He tossed it in a nearby wastebasket. "Part of why I'd asked Mr. Abora to seek out a baker was to help my son's business."

"There's no way Julian would let me work for him," Lillie said with an incredulous laugh.

"Well, he might not have a choice. See, he may own the carafes and plates and cups, but I'm still the owner of the building. I do get some say in what he does and doesn't do." He tapped his finger to his chin. "And, of course, I could *highly* encourage my tenants to forego their morning pastry at the Globe Café in favor of the Pobyd Perfections Bakery if he declined."

Lillie's heart skipped a beat. "Really?"

"*If* he declines," Mr. Globe said. "But I think it's better for everyone if you and Julian join forces. He's not meant to be up at the crack of dawn, mixing batter and making bread dough. He's a

Globe, and he should be here with me, running the business."

"I...see..." Lillie said slowly.

"I know you've put a lot of time and effort into your bakery," Mr. Globe said. "And I can appreciate that you've made yourself at home there. But you haven't had many customers, I assume. The fisherfolk are wonderful, but they don't seem to appreciate the finer things in life like those who live on this side of Silverkeep. If you took over the café, you'd have more business than you knew what to do with."

"So if I understand you," Lillie said, "you're saying that you'll convince your son Julian to give up the bakery so I can take it over. And you'd want me to close my bakery near the wharf to run the Globe Café?"

"And move apartments, too," he said. "Julian lives above the Silverkeep Café now, but I'm sure it wouldn't take much to convince him to leave. Both could be yours for...ten gold coins a month."

Lillie narrowed her gaze. "But if I stayed in my current location, I'd have to pay Rey Moussison half a chocolate chip cookie every day. No gold to you at all." She paused, watching his expression carefully. "Because, as we've established, you're not the owner of my building. So I wouldn't be paying you anything."

"Sugar and flour are expensive," Mr. Globe said.

"I hear Garwood Calcut has been procuring you chocolate and other things you need. If you're making things only to throw them away, you'll soon be out of gold. Then you won't even have enough to make Mr. Moussison's half a cookie."

"I'm sure word will get out," Lillie said. "And I'm happy to take customers off Julian's hands, should he decide that baking is no longer what he wants to do. Because I sincerely doubt he's going to give up his bakery to me, of all people."

"If you'll agree to move, in addition to encouraging my tenants to visit your shop, I'll also hire you to make a cake for a gathering we're about to have. One that would get your skills in front of nearly every person who lives on the north side of town."

"I'm listening."

"Kemp will be revealing his grand plan for the town," Mr. Globe said. "Who gets to stay, who'll have to relocate elsewhere in the town. We plan on holding a town meeting tomorrow afternoon, and I'd like to hire you to make a cake for that event—one that would feed everyone." He paused. "Assuming, of course, we have a deal on the rest of it."

Lillie took a deep breath. Moving from the empty southern part of town to the northern one seemed a no-brainer. There were more people, and folks clearly wanted sweets, so there was a need for it. She'd have no problem selling out of every pastry she made, becoming as busy as she'd been back in Pigsend with Allen. As far as Julian was concerned, Lillie had no doubts a man as ruthless as Mr. Globe would squeeze his son by any means necessary to get him to acquiesce to his demands. And all Lillie would have to do was pack her meager things and move...

...leaving behind the display case Earl had made for her, and the table. The curtains Etheldra had picked out for the apartment. The painted walls and *Pobyd Perfections* on the window. Ursil would have to come up the hill for his morning pastry, and the market would be farther away. The Kovens would, presumably, still have to fork over two gold coins every month—and Lillie would have to pay Mr. Globe ten, perhaps an easy feat assuming the client base continued to patronize her at the Globe Café. But she'd have to leave behind Rey, who might still have to fight this fight with Mr. Globe when the next tenant moved in.

"I need to think about it," she said, after a moment. "It's a big ask."

"I don't think there's much to think about," he said. "A ready-made bakery with ready-made customers willing and excited to buy whatever you dream up. Seems like a win-win to me."

"It is tempting, for sure, but I shouldn't make hasty decisions," Lillie said. "I am, of course, willing to bake your cake for the town meeting." She paused with a smile. "On the house, too. Can't pass up an opportunity to advertise to the entire town, now, can I?"

His eyes darkened.

"You know, if I make something delicious enough, I might get to keep the bakery *and* those customers you were talking about," Lillie said, tapping her chin. "And not have to move anywhere at all."

"I would think about—"

"I will give your offer serious thought," Lillie said, rising. "But it's time for me to get back to the bakery. I'm sure there's a line of customers in need of a non-burnt muffin."

Chapter Eighteen

As a general rule, Lillie didn't like going toe to toe with people, but the more time she spent in Mr. Globe's presence, the more defiant she became. He treated her like he had all the power, but he didn't. He was just a man, and even though he had plenty of influence, there was nothing that said he controlled *everything* in town. Lillie was an excellent baker, and she didn't need him to send customers her way.

Yet, as the day wore on, and no customers came to the bakery, Lillie started to wonder if that was true.

"This is outrageous," Rey said, standing in the display case window. "You have all this delicious food. I *know* they see it. Why aren't they coming in?"

"They're busy, I suppose," Lillie said. "On the clock with their rich bosses in the north. Probably can't stop in to grab a muffin while they're at work."

"You don't seem worried," Rey said, climbing out of the front window. "And you seem different since you got back from Mr. Globe. What did he say?"

"I've been hired to make a cake for the town meeting," Lillie said, instead of the truth. "Though I don't exactly know what kind. Or how many people I should be feeding. Maybe I should ask Mr. Abora about it." She paused. "Mr. Globe says he's almost finished with the grand plan for the town, whatever that means."

"It means a lot of people are about to be really upset," Rey replied. "No wonder he wanted you to make something sweet."

"I'm glad it seems to be coming to an end," Lillie said. "The last few times I've been at the town hall, it's been awful. Everyone's angry at Mr. Abora."

"I mean, I don't blame them," Rey replied. "Not that I don't love you and the Kovens as tenants, but he didn't even *ask* me. I've actually never spoken to the man. So it doesn't seem to me that he cares that much for property rights. Maybe you should've been talking with *him* instead of Mr. Globe."

"I think Mr. Abora assumed, like all the others, you'd been arrested," Lillie said. "The queen's laws were clear on the matter, but that doesn't mean they were right."

"Yes, but *I* never left," Rey said. "Mr. Abora never stopped long enough to look for me. But that's typical of you larger set. My many-times great grandfather used to say that you had to speak up if you wanted to be heard."

Lillie would've liked to have seen a mouse stand up in the town hall and demand to be taken seriously.

"Well, last time I went to the town hall, the line to speak with Mr. Abora was out the door," Lillie said. "Even if I went now, there's no guarantee I'd get in to speak with him anytime soon."

"Catch him on his way to dinner, then," Rey said. "I know from Lenoire Rattington—she lives at the inn and helps out with the crumbs and such the guests leave behind—that Mr. Abora dines there almost every evening. I'm sure if you showed up, he'd have no choice but to talk with you."

"Do you think?" Lillie said, smiling. "Maybe I'll bring him a little sweet to have for dessert, too. He seemed to like the cupcake I brought."

"Couldn't hurt," Rey said. "And in the meantime, I'll see what I can find out on my end."

"On your end?" Lillie asked.

"Yes," he said with a solemn nod. "The Mouse Whisper Network is vast in this town. Lots of ears and lots of tongues. If someone's out there writing letters and threatening people, I'm sure the rumor mill is churning." He hopped between his feet in excitement. "Oh, this is fun. I think we're going to make an excellent team, Lillie."

The sun was setting when Lillie locked up and headed up the hill with a chocolate cupcake. Rey had already left, eager to pump his own network of mice and other small creatures for information. He was a curious fellow, Lillie decided, and she didn't mind him being around. If anything, it gave her someone to talk to. And seeing as he did seem to know a *lot* about things in the city, he might come in handy as she navigated this new life.

Which, once again, made her think twice about Mr. Globe's offer. To leave Rey and the rest seemed… Well, it didn't really seem right to Lillie. Something about getting into business with Mr. Globe gave her serious pause.

As Rey had said, she spotted the assistant mayor hurrying across the street to the Silverkeep Inn, keeping his head down and his pace brisk. Perhaps he was worried someone might follow him, but no one else was on the street.

Lillie pressed on, walking through the front

door of the inn and taking stock of things. The dining room was twice the size of the one back at the Weary Dragon, and the patrons seemed to be the upper crust of Silverkeep. She recognized a few people from the town hall crowd—mostly ones who'd been vehement about keeping their existing spots. But Benetta was there, too; unsurprisingly, as she was probably still staying at the inn until the mess with her shop was sorted. She sat at a small table in the corner with Mr. Roudie, who had obviously bathed and spiffed himself up.

Benetta caught sight of Lillie and glared at her, but Lillie turned in the other direction. She wasn't keen on having another discussion with the seamstress, not when she had more pressing matters.

She looked around the room but didn't see Mr. Abora. He'd definitely gone inside; she'd watched him walk through the door. She scanned the room more closely but still didn't see him. Noemi caught her gaze and beckoned her over.

"Here for dinner?" she asked. "It's one silver. But there's not much left, I'm afraid. You'll have to come earlier."

"I'm looking for Mr. Abora," Lillie said. "I saw him walk in. But I don't see him in the dining room. Has he already left?"

She clicked her tongue. "Mr. Abora dines privately these days."

"Ah." Lillie could understand that. "Is there any

chance he might see me?" She lifted the pastry box. "I, erm, have a gift. Thought he could use a pick-me-up after all the yelling."

Noemi didn't seem to believe her. "He's asked me to put off anyone who asks to see him."

"Well, then…" Lillie pushed the box toward her. "Could you please deliver this to him?"

She inspected the box as if it were poison but pulled it toward herself. Then, without a word, she disappeared into the kitchen.

"Thank you," Lillie muttered, turning to leave but running right into a broad chest. She looked up into the scowling face of Julian Globe.

"Watch where you're going," he snapped, reaching around her to deposit his dirty plate on the counter.

"So sorry," Lillie said, more nicely than she felt.

"What are you doing here?" he said. "Shouldn't you be down south tending to your bakery?"

"I brought a gift to Mr. Abora," Lillie said thinly.

"Why? Trying to bribe him?"

"No, actually," Lillie said, putting her hands on her hips. "This may be a foreign concept to you, but it's clear to me he's had a rough couple of days. Thought he could use something sweet to cheer him up."

"He's been getting plenty of sweets at my shop," Julian said with a glare. "Doesn't need any of yours."

Lillie clicked her tongue, ready to tell Julian that his father was plotting against him, but before she could, Noemi reappeared from the back.

"You. Pobyd. Mr. Abora says you can go back."

Julian glowered at her as heat rose in Lillie's cheeks. "What?"

"Just a nice gift, hm? No ulterior motive?" he said.

"Yes, a nice gift," Lillie said, inching away from him. "Now if you'll excuse me…"

Lillie ducked behind the innkeeper to the kitchen, where she found Mr. Abora eating his meal at Noemi's kitchen table. The cupcake was gone, and there were flecks of chocolate on his cheeks as he waved her over.

"Come, come," he said. "Thank you so much for that. It really hit the spot."

"Glad you liked it," Lillie said, pulling the other stool out from under the table and sitting. "And thank you for letting me chat with you for a minute."

He sighed, wearily, and dark bags hung under his eyes. "Don't tell me something's amiss with the bakery…"

"Yes, but we've sorted it," Lillie said.

"Thank goodness. I've got enough on my plate dealing with the angry crowd sleeping in the town hall." He blew air between his lips. "Just a nightmare, really. Had I known what was coming down the pike, what with all the magical folks coming out of the woodwork again, I never would've agreed to invite people to town."

"It's not your fault," Lillie said. "You couldn't have imagined the king would come back to power."

"Not in our wildest dreams," he said. "That's what makes it all so difficult. Obviously, I want to be fair to those who had to flee for their own safety. But I also have to be fair to the folks who've moved in."

"Understandable," Lillie said. "I hear you've got a big plan, though, right? Going to reveal it in a town meeting in a few days?"

"How did you—?"

"Word travels," Lillie said with a shrug. "I thought it might be a good opportunity for me to advertise a little, if you're willing."

The blank look on his face told her Mr. Globe hadn't been in communication with him. That was a good sign. "Advertise?"

"The bakery isn't quite as busy as I'd hoped," Lillie said. "Don't get me wrong, I'm happy to be where I am. The folks down at the fish market are some of the nicest I've met, and the Kovens have certainly made me feel welcome. But…it seems people still have their reservations about me. So, I thought it would be nice to make something for the town. Really put everyone in a good mood."

"You aren't going to...put anything in it, are you?"

Lillie blanched. "What do you mean?"

"I mean, I did a little research on pobyds," he said. "Apparently, you can...well, influence people if you put your minds to it."

"We can, but I don't think the citizens of Silverkeep would appreciate that," Lillie said with a tight smile. "I'd rather bake them something delicious and put them in a good mood that way. I won't charge anything, of course. Just happy to have the opportunity to share what I can do."

Before he could respond, the back door opened. "*There* you are!"

Maire Gaides, the seamstress who lived in Benetta's shop, stormed through the kitchen door, closing it behind her. Mr. Abora wilted, perhaps wondering if he should've paid Noemi more money to keep the angry townsfolk at bay.

"Maire, I told you I'd be happy to talk with you in the morning," Mr. Abora said. "But you'll have to wait your turn—"

"Then why is *she* here?" Maire said, pointing at Lillie.

"I'm here delivering cupcakes and discussing cakes for the town meeting," Lillie said, holding up her hands innocently.

"This can't wait, Mr. Abora. I'm being *hounded* by that monstrous Benetta Pearlson."

"Yes, Maire," Mr. Abora said. "I understand. I've told her that we're working on a solution, but—"

"She's relentless. Every *one* of those monsters are. I'm about to hire someone to sit on my front stoop and keep all of them from darkening my door." Maire huffed, glaring at Lillie. "You're her friend, aren't you? Tell her to back off."

"I wouldn't call us friends," Lillie said. "What's she doing?"

"She's being... Well, she's contacting all my clients and telling them that if they patronize my shop again, they'll be showing disloyalty to Silverkeep. As if *I* haven't been here, loyally serving the people, while she's been off who-knows-where. I'm terribly sorry for what happened to her. I truly am. But that's no excuse to harass me to the point of black—" She stopped suddenly, as if she wanted to say something, but didn't.

Lillie eyed her suspiciously. *Had Maire received a letter?*

"I promise, I'll have a talk with her," Mr. Abora said wearily. "And when Sheriff Juno returns, she'll do the same. Everyone's unsettled right now, but I promise, we will sort all this out. We'll find a way to make everyone happy at the town meeting."

That certainly seemed like a bridge too far to Lillie, and based on Maire's expression, she thought so, too. "I will be happy when Benetta stops trying to ruin my business." She turned stiffly. "And as *you* invited me here, I expect *you* to do something about it."

"I promise, I am," he said.

She turned to leave, huffing away, and Lillie watched her go curiously. She doubted the seamstress would talk to her, or admit to receiving a letter, but it did add a new wrinkle to things. So far, Lillie had assumed someone was out to get her and the Kovens, but what if someone was targeting *everyone* Mr. Abora had invited?

"So sorry about that," Mr. Abora said. "So you want to bake a cake for the town meeting tomorrow?"

~

Lillie finished chatting with Mr. Abora about the cake specifications (no preference on flavor, to be delivered at ten o'clock tomorrow morning) then let herself out the back door. She wasn't keen on running into Julian, nor did she want to be seen by Benetta or anyone else. But she didn't head back to the bakery right away, not when she had new questions about these mysterious letters. Someone not only knew about Lillie's past in Silverkeep, but Nikola's nymph magic *and* Maire's…whatever her secret was. The first thing would be to confirm that Maire *had*, in fact, received a written threat. Maybe that would uncover another clue as to who might be behind them.

Lillie briefly considered Benetta as a suspect

again. There was plenty of motivation for Benetta to want Maire to leave town, and she definitely knew Lillie's secret, but the Kovens? Lillie doubted Benetta even knew who they were. They certainly added an interesting twist to the entire situation.

She ducked around the inn to the town square, now bathed in moonlight. All the shops and offices were closed, but there was one light on across the way. Maire stood in the front window of her shop, clearly talking with someone as she gestured wildly. Lillie was turning to leave when the very mysterious Mr. Calcut crossed in front of the window.

"Probably nothing," Lillie muttered. "Mr. Calcut's a merchant. Surely, he finds fabric for seamstresses, too."

But something drew her closer, a curiosity she couldn't ignore. And when she got close enough to hear fragments of their conversation, she was glad she'd listened to her gut.

"The magical people are back, aren't they? I want a protection spell. Put it on every window and door so no one with any magic can cross it." Maire huffed. "If Benetta Pearlson thinks she can threaten me with a nasty letter, she's got another think coming!"

Chapter Nineteen

I knew it!

Lillie maneuvered until she found a spot she could stay hidden and still hear. Maire was going on about the type of protection she wanted, and Mr. Calcut seemed bored by the entire conversation.

"That will take some time," he said, lazily. "Why don't you ask Lucia Guilly?"

"I want magic," Maire said.

"Then I hear Greeley Sloos is back." His tone was observational. "He could make you a repelling potion."

"I don't want... It's one of *those* people

threatening me," Maire said. "The ones who think they have a right to our property. I'm sure they're all in cahoots, sharing people's secrets and figuring out the most underhanded way to steal what was rightfully given."

"What kind of threat are we talking about?" Mr. Calcut asked, eyeing her. "Perhaps this is a conversation better left with Sheriff Juno."

"No one knows where she is," Maire said. "And besides that…" She looked uncomfortable, and Lillie narrowed her gaze suspiciously. "Well, there's no need to involve her when I can fix the problem myself."

"So you want a spell that will repel all magical creatures," he said. "You realize that might mean some of your clients won't be able to come into your store."

She scoffed. "*My* clients don't have magic."

Mr. Calcut made a noise, and Lillie had to wonder how many secrets *he* was hiding. He turned toward Lillie, and for a brief, terrifying moment, Lillie thought he'd spotted her. But if he had, he had no reaction as he counted the doors and windows.

"It's going to be a hefty price," he said. "Three gold coins for the amount of potion you'd need."

"*Three* gold coins?" Maire sputtered. "Are you out of your mind? I'm not paying—"

"You are, of course, welcome to seek out other

merchants."

Silence hung in the air, and Lillie waited for Maire to argue with him.

"When can you get me the potion?" she asked, sounding like she'd eaten something sour.

"For another silver, I'm sure I can find something by morning," he said, flashing her a greedy smile.

"Fine." Maire reached into a coin purse at her side and yanked out three gold pieces and a silver. "I suppose it's worth it to get a good night's sleep. I don't trust that Benetta Pearlson not to hire someone to cast a curse on me. Probably the next step if I don't…"

"Leave," Lillie whispered to herself.

Mr. Calcut took the coins, counted the windows again, then tipped his hat to her. "I'll be back at sunup."

With that, he walked out into the darkness, all but disappearing in the scant light. Lillie held her breath as he passed, waiting for him to say something, but he kept walking. Lillie turned back to Maire, who stood on the stoop of her shop. The seamstress scanned the town square, her brows knitted and her arms wrapped tightly around herself. Then, with a *humph*, she slammed the door shut.

Lillie spent most of the night awake, thinking

about what secrets Maire had, as well as who might know them. Not only that, but had anyone else gotten a letter, too? Was it all about trying to get people to leave Silverkeep?

If so, the list of suspects had both narrowed and grown. Had a newly-returned person written them, hoping to scare the transplants instead of waiting for Mr. Abora to come up with a plan?

When four in the morning arrived, Lillie rose groggily but headed downstairs to stoke the fires in her oven anyway. She had a cake to bake, one that would hopefully introduce her to the town and pique their interest enough to sway them from Globe Café. She'd been so distracted by what she'd seen at Maire's that she hadn't given the recipe any thought at all. She had picked up half a dozen lemons the other day, so a three-tiered lemon cake with lemon buttercream icing would do the trick. She'd have to make it in batches, as she only had enough butter, milk and eggs to make half of it before Kristin arrived. But she could still get it all done before ten.

She started by making her butter with her remaining milk, which she then creamed with the sugar. While that worked, she sifted together flour, salt, and leavening, encouraging the latter to be light and fluffy. This cake would be bursting with flavor, and part of what made it delicious was the airy texture. When the butter and sugar were fully creamed, Lillie added eggs one at a time then the rest of the milk, and finally, very slowly, the dry mixture.

Then she took four lemons, using her grater to scrape all the zest off. She whispered to the lemons to be sour and delicious, then cut them open and squeezed the juice into the batter, holding the lemons over the palm of her hand to catch the seeds. She set her spoon to start mixing that while she assembled her baking pans.

She had three large cake pans and three smaller ones to make two of her three tiers, and she buttered and floured them so they wouldn't stick. When her mixture was well-combined, she added an equal amount to each pan, scraping the bottom of the bowl to get the last small tin filled.

Just as she was fitting the last tin in the oven, the back door opened and Kristin walked in, carrying another crate of milk and eggs.

"Perfect timing," Lillie said with a smile. "Help yourself to anything in the front display case. Just bring it here first so I can freshen it up a bit."

"What smells so good?" Kristin asked, crossing the kitchen to find something in the shop.

"Lemon cake, for the town meeting later today," Lillie said.

Kristin returned with a chocolate chip scone, and with a suggestion from Lillie, the confection warmed and softened up as if it had just come out of the oven. The dairy farmer sat on Lillie's kitchen stool and took a bite, sighing happily.

"Town meeting? What kind of town meeting?"

Lillie stopped and looked at her. "You don't have regular town meetings in Silverkeep?"

"Not that I'm aware of. But I'm not *technically* a Silverkeep resident, so perhaps I don't get the invitation."

"Ah." Lillie supposed that made sense. "Mr. Abora's going to reveal his plan for the newly-returned and the transplants. I offered to bake a cake to make everyone happy." She looked at the lemons in the crate. Should be enough to finish off the last tiers. "Thought it was a good opportunity to showcase what I can do." She chewed her lips. "Business hasn't been that steady. I'm not sure Ursil's powers of persuasion are working, to be honest."

"All they need is one taste of this," Kristin said, lifting the scone in the air. "Then they'll be customers for life, like me."

Lillie certainly hoped that was true. She made the second round of cake batter and stuffed that in the oven while the first round cooled. While that worked, she busied herself with a strawberry-rhubarb custard to fill in tartlets, and cast a freshening spell over what she could sell, and removed the things too old to revive, which were far too many for her liking.

"This has to work," Lillie muttered, moving things around to be more presentable. "This really has to work. I don't want to move. Nor do I want to work for *him*."

"What has to work?"

Lillie jumped and spun. Rey stood at the mouth of his mousehole, rubbing his whiskers and looking like he'd rather be back in bed.

"Morning," Lillie said. "I didn't see you last night when I got back."

"Oh, it was a late night for me." He scampered to the display case and climbed up. "I got caught chatting with Lenoire at the inn. She'd gotten a nip of ale, and we were reminiscing about when a ship full of chocolate was stranded here due to a broken sail." He sighed. "Needless to say, we were quite well fed that week."

"I can imagine," Lillie said.

"But you said something needed to work?" Rey asked. "Also, all this talk of chocolate has made me hungry for a cookie."

Lillie broke off half a chocolate chip cookie in the display case and handed it to him. "There's a town meeting today. I'm baking a multi-tiered cake to show off what I can do, hopefully to get more customers." She looked at the bakery, a little forlornly. "I'm not sure I'll get an opportunity like that again, you know?"

"You mentioned working for *him*," Rey said, the

chocolate chip cookie bulging in his cheek. "Who were you talking about?"

Lillie sank onto the stool. "Mr. Globe asked me to take over the Globe Café."

Rey stopped chewing. "He...what?"

"He thinks he can convince Julian to give it up, which I don't believe," Lillie said. "And he said I could move into the apartment above the bakery, too. But I'd be paying *him* ten gold coins every month. And probably...be working for him. I don't love that idea. Something about him gives me the creeps."

"Absolutely not!" Rey said. "I forbid it. You simply *must* stay. Where am I going to get my cookies?" He gestured to the shop. "And you worked so hard to make this place pretty. You'd give it up?"

"I'm not sure I have much of a choice," Lillie said. "Mr. Globe made it sound like if I declined his offer, he'd encourage his tenants, which includes most of the town, to avoid my shop. We didn't get a *single* person in yesterday. Can't help but feel like he's tightening the screws a bit."

"He's cross because you found out he didn't own the place," Rey said. "I do hope you've informed him the Kovens won't be paying either."

Lillie demurred, instead telling Rey about the cake Mr. Globe had offered to pay for if she agreed to his deal, which she was now making for free in hopes of bypassing him and reaching customers directly.

"I'm honestly not sure why he brought it up," Lillie said. "Seems like an oversight."

"You'd better tread carefully, Lillie," Rey said. "Audo Globe didn't get to where he is because he makes mistakes. The things the Mouse Whisper Network could tell you about him…"

Lillie chewed her lip. "Do you think he'd send blackmail letters to get people to move out?"

"I wouldn't put it past him," Rey said. "Why?"

"A few people have gotten letters telling them to leave or else they'll reveal some damaging secrets," Lillie said. "I wonder if Mr. Globe isn't sending them to make space for the people who've returned."

"Who's gotten one?" Rey surveyed her.

Lillie didn't feel comfortable telling chatty Rey about hers or the Kovens letter yet. "Maire Gaides. She was up in arms last night about being threatened and wanting to keep all the magical people out."

"That makes sense," Rey said with a nod. "Maire has quite the secret."

Lillie started. "What do you mean?"

He bounced on his hind legs, like he was eager to spill something he shouldn't. "*Apparently*, Kemp Abora didn't have to do much convincing for Maire to move to Silverkeep. She was in desperate need of a new town, having had an *affair* with the married mayor. And not only that, the two of them had taken all kinds of vacations on the city's dime. Just scandal after scandal. The Mouse Whisper Network was absolutely ablaze with it when she moved to town."

"Certainly something someone wouldn't want shared," Lillie said, though she felt bad that it seemed every mouse in town knew Maire's secret. "You said the Mouse Whisper Network knows everything, right?"

"If we don't, we could surely find out," he said with a nod.

"Have you heard any rumors about...my past?" Lillie asked. Maybe the puzzle piece she was missing was a very small one with large ears and a penchant for gossip.

"Can't say I have," he said, taking a step forward. "Did you get a letter, too, Lillie?"

After a moment's hesitation, she nodded. "I think I was the first. Then...Ursil got one."

He gasped and jumped backward. "Perfidy! I won't stand for *that*. The Kovens have absolutely nothing to hide! What could they possibly fear?" He rubbed his snout. "Well, maybe the fisherfolk wouldn't like it if they knew Nikola was a nymph. Is that it?"

Lillie didn't love how quickly he'd jumped to that. "Erm. I don't want to—"

"We've known Nikola was a nymph for *ages*," he said, waving her off. "The mice don't care." He stepped forward again. "But you must be hiding some secret. You're already living openly with magic, so it's not that."

"I made a mistake," Lillie said.

"What kind of mistake?"

"One that would've endangered a lot of people, had I been successful," Lillie said. "I was a bit desperate, living in Lower Pigsend—"

"Mm!" Reynard snapped his claws together. "You're *that* pobyd. The one who stole the talisman from Lower Pigsend!"

Lillie's mouth fell open. "What? How did you…?"

"My cousins were down there, remember?" Reynard said, scampering over as if he'd uncovered buried treasure. "Said there was this big brouhaha with some pobyd who'd stolen the protective talisman keeping the town safe from the queen. She didn't break the spell but came close to it. Got kicked out and no one really knew what happened to her." His whiskers twitched. "I can't believe I didn't put two and two together!"

Lillie's face paled. "Erm…"

"Huh." He sat back, eyeing her. "You don't look like the kind of person to do that."

"Well, I…did." Admitting it didn't make her feel much better, but it was preferable to lying. "I'm not proud of it. And I had to rebuild my life while avoiding the queen's soldiers. Now I'm here and…"

Rey scrutinized her. "You know, I never actually enrolled at Sheepsburg University. I never paid any tuition or made the professors aware I was there. I tell people I graduated, but I was never tested on anything, so I don't think it counts."

Lillie gave him a sideways look. "What does that have to do with anything?"

"I'm saying, we all have things we aren't proud of," he said. "So if the worst thing you can say is that you *almost* broke a spell, but you came to your senses…"

"I mean, that's not all I did," Lillie said. "I also infused some cookies with a sleeping intention on a dear friend so I could try to break the spell in his living room without him being the wiser." She paused, but since they were getting everything out in the open. "And very recently, I made a truth-intention jam and almost gave it to Benetta when I thought she was the one sending the letters."

"Well, why didn't you let her eat it? Seems like that would've solved all the problems right then and there," he said.

"Yes, except I'm sure she would've noticed, and based on my past history in Lower Pigsend, she might've spread a rumor around town to make my business even worse than it is," Lillie said. "I don't think people want to visit a shop where they might be forced to spill their secrets."

"*Or* you'd have lines out the door," Rey said, excitedly. "I know I'd like to have a cookie like that. I have a cousin who lies like they breathe. One drop of that jam, and he'd tell me exactly where he hid my gold watch." His whiskers twitched. "What other kinds of magic can you infuse in your goods?"

"The magic to make things delicious," Lillie said. "Which is all I want to do." She glanced at the clock. "My first batch of sponges is probably cool enough now to ice, and I've got to get it assembled so I can bring it up the hill later today."

"Fair enough." He picked up another piece of cookie. "If it will help, I can ask around the network to see if anyone's heard of anyone else getting letters. Or if anyone knows who you are."

"Erm..." Lillie cleared her throat. "You won't... tell anyone my secret, will you? I know the smaller folk might not interact with the bigger ones, but--"

"I'm not *that* bad of a gossip," Rey said, pushing another large chunk of cookie to the side of his mouth. "You can trust me, Lillie. Why would I want to ruin the life of my personal baker?"

Chapter Twenty

Rey left shortly after that, vowing to press his network of mice and other small creatures to find out what he could about the letters. The final tiers of sponges were ready to come out of the oven, and Lillie coaxed the heat to dissipate faster so she could get to icing. She couldn't quite concentrate, though, her mind spinning with fears that her past was about to be revealed to the entire city. But while Rey was a gossip, he seemed to know there were things that shouldn't be shared. He'd made a good point about Nikola, and also about her feeding him.

"Suppose it's good luck I'm a baker and not a

cobbler," Lillie muttered to herself.

Still, someone out there *did* know her secret, and Lillie was bound and determined to figure out who it was. She briefly entertained the idea of adding something special to the buttercream icing, but dismissed it immediately. This cake was to be her introduction to the town, and she wanted her baking to speak for itself.

Once the tiers were cool, she assembled them on her cake pedestal into three tiers of three layers each, with a generous dollop of lemon buttercream icing between each layer then added an even layer of thin icing around both tiers to serve as the barrier between the crumby sponge and the outer decor. She turned the cake on the pedestal to visualize how she wanted to pipe the rest of the buttercream on. She started with the star tip, then created little puffs around the edge of the top and middle tiers. Then she piped the same style along the bottom tier where it met the pedestal.

"You know," she said to no one, "if I had a bit more time, I'd have made some candied lemon peels." She glanced at the clock. "Next time."

With the sun being as warm as it had been, Lillie wanted to get the cake up the hill and into the town hall well before ten. It was heavy, but Lillie was used to carrying heavy things, and she took her time navigating the cobblestones as she climbed the hill, whispering encouragement for the buttercream to hold and the tiers to stay together.

As she approached the town hall, she realized with a start that she'd run into a problem. The front doors were closed, and she needed a hand free to open them. She looked around, hoping someone might be on the street to give her a hand, when blessedly, the doors opened.

Her heart sank to her stomach as Julian Globe walked out.

"What is *that*?"

"A very heavy cake," Lillie said with a smile. "Would you mind getting the door for me?"

"I would, actually," he said. "Why do you have that?"

"It's for the town meeting," Lillie said.

"Who asked you to make it?"

"No one—Goodness, Julian, can you stop being a sourpuss for one minute and help me?"

He flung open the door, and Lillie scrambled up the steps, her arms starting to hurt from the effort of carrying the cake. She stepped inside, finding the room absolutely packed and echoing with murmuring and conversations. But what stopped her wasn't the crowd, which she'd somewhat expected.

It was the other multi-tiered cake sitting on the front table.

"I asked because I was *also* asked to make a cake for the occasion," Julian said, standing behind her.

"By my father."

Lillie scowled. *That little...* Rey had warned her that Audo Globe wasn't to be trusted. "I see. Well, great minds think alike, I suppose." She forced a smile onto her face. "Besides that, more cake is always a good thing. Now there's plenty for everyone."

"I doubt *anyone* will want to touch that," Julian glared at the other cake. "No telling what you put in it."

"What I..." Lillie turned, which was a feat considering the weight she was carrying. "I put nothing in this cake but flour, sugar, butter, egg, leavening, and lemon juice."

"No magic?" He quirked a brow.

"I may have encouraged it to stay together on the walk here, but that's it," Lillie said, a little hastily. "I don't know if you've heard, but magic isn't illegal anymore. So if you'll excuse me, I'm going to put this very heavy cake down so the rest of the town can enjoy it."

She kept walking up the center aisle, feeling the gazes of everyone in the room on her. Well, she'd wanted notoriety. This wasn't the best way to go about it, but perhaps she could still salvage this event. With a sigh, she placed the lemon cake on the table next to Julian's. Up close, she could see an attempt at decorative icing, but it paled in comparison to hers. Even after its trek from the bakery, Lillie's was still in pristine condition.

She turned to the crowd, unsure when or how they would want to eat, and couldn't help but notice that no one was meeting her gaze. A few people were whispering and pointing, enough that Lillie couldn't help but feel she was already well-known, and not for a good reason.

She wiped her hands on her apron and sought out a friendly face. Wineke and her partner Greeley were sitting on the end of one of the benches, so Lillie marched over, hoping to get some insight into what everyone was saying about her.

"Wineke, hi." Lillie smiled. "How's it going?"

"Oh, hi, Lillie." She looked a little uncomfortable. "Erm. I see you brought a cake."

"Yes. Please tell me you're going to have some," Lillie said, gesturing to the front table. "Julian's got one up there, but I daresay mine's going to be much more delicious."

Wineke once again looked uncomfortable, glancing at her partner for a moment. He turned to look up at Lillie with a stone-cold glare.

"We don't want to be mind-controlled, thanks."

Lillie's mouth fell open as her heart dipped to her stomach. "*Mind-controlled?* What are you talking about?"

"We heard that you're keen on putting magical persuasion into your cakes and pastries," Greeley continued. "Wineke was feeling all kinds of good when she ate those cookies."

"That's because they're delicious," Lillie said. "I didn't add any magic, let alone magic that could sway you to do anything…"

But her anger was boiling over, and she found the person who'd been spreading awful rumors about her sitting a few rows behind. She balled her fists as she stormed over, breathing heavily out of her nose.

"What's the big idea, Benetta?" Lillie barked.

"I'm *sure* I don't know what you mean," Benetta replied, looking up at her.

"Are you the one who's told everyone I'm some kind of…some kind of *mind controller*?" Lillie sputtered.

She put her hand to her chest, smirking. "I mean, if the shoe fits—" Lillie saw red and took a step toward her, but the seamstress put up her hands in surrender. "I heard the rumor, but it wasn't me. Seems like it started over on *that* side of the world." She thumbed toward the transplant side of the town hall. "Perhaps someone making up lies to besmirch all of us. Wouldn't be surprised."

Lillie turned to the other side, where she spotted Maire and others she'd seen around town. The only person she'd ever had an extended conversation with was Noemi, and she couldn't imagine the innkeeper spreading nasty rumors. But as she surveyed the room, she spotted the second cake at the front of the room and knew immediately where the rumor had come from.

"What's your problem with me?"

The Globe Café was, for once, empty of customers, as everyone was in the town hall, waiting for Mr. Abora's big announcement. Julian was in the kitchen, mixing a batter of some kind. His sleeves were rolled up, revealing thick arms, and his apron was well-loved with smears of chocolate and jam. When Lillie stormed in, he looked up and glared then went back to his baking.

"I asked you a question," Lillie said, marching right back into the kitchen. "I've done nothing to hurt you. And yet... Yet you're spreading nasty rumors about me. Saying that I cast spells in my pastries to influence people."

"Then what was in that jam?"

Lillie stopped short. "What are you talking about?"

"The jam that was on those cookies you brought to the Silverkeep Inn," he said. "I saw the whole thing. You'd given them to that dock repairman to bring to Benetta Pearlson, but took them away again. They landed on the floor."

"I threw them away," Lillie said, narrowing her eyes. "Don't tell me you...picked one out of the waste bin and ate it."

"The how and why don't matter," he said, his

cheeks darkening. "The point is, there was *something* in those cookies that made me feel like I needed to tell everyone my deepest secrets. And you were going to serve them to the folks at the Silverkeep Inn. You're dangerous."

"Couple things." Lillie crossed her arms. "One, I was going to serve them to Benetta, and Benetta alone, because I thought she was lying to me about something important. Two...*you ate cookies from my trash?*" She narrowed her gaze. "And finally, what do you have against the Kovens?"

"Who's that?"

"My neighbors. They also received a nasty letter," Lillie said. "Clearly, you're the one sending them. You also sent one to Maire Gaides and who knows who else. Trying to improve your father's opinion of you by clearing out some folks who need a home?"

"Yeah, you'd know all about my father, wouldn't you?" He dumped a handful of blueberries into the batter. "I heard all about your little *meeting* the other day. Barging your way onto his calendar to tell him you wanted *my* café."

"I didn't... Well." She wasn't sure how to explain Rey. "I did get onto his calendar. But *he* offered *me* your café."

Julian's eyes widened a fraction as he stopped stirring.

"It turns out he doesn't actually own my

building," she said. "So I went to clear the air about that. While I was there, he mentioned he wanted me to take over your bakery and your apartment. If you ask me, I think he wanted to keep collecting rent from me because that seems to be the only thing he cares about." She lifted her chin. "In any case, I have my doubts that he'd be able to extract you from the Globe Café, and I *also* have my doubts about being in business with him."

Julian worked his jaw, and some of the hard lines she'd become accustomed to loosened.

"You very clearly have a lot of pride in your bakery," Lillie said. "And while... Well, I don't think it's a surprise that I think your skills need a bit of brushing up, but you make a good go of it. I meant what I said when we first met: I'm not interested in being your competition." She sighed with a smile. "I love my bakery. I love the location. And I love the people down by the wharf. I'm not looking to move." She swallowed, looking back at the town hall. "But it turns out I may have to leave anyway, because of the rumor you started about me. I haven't had a customer in days. And I doubt anyone's going to want to have any of the cake I spent hours making to impress them."

She turned to him, pleased to see he looked remorseful.

"Well, that's that." Lillie swallowed. "Suppose I should head back to my bakery to start packing things up. At least in Pigsend, they don't think I'm a monster."

"I didn't write any letters to any of you," Julian said, as she was almost to the door. "Not to you or your neighbors or whoever else you mentioned. All I did was start the rumor. And for that... I'm sorry."

Lillie shut the door behind her.

Lillie sat behind her display case, inspecting everything from the grain of the wood to the faint brushstrokes. She did the same to her kitchen table. There was no way she'd be able to bring both with her. With the gold she still had, she could get back to Pigsend, but there wouldn't be much left after that. She'd have to bake a ton of scones to use up the remainder of her flour and sugar, or she could leave it with...well, not Julian. He'd done enough.

How *dare* he spread rumors about her? But if she hadn't been so foolhardy as to make those cookies in the first place, he wouldn't have had anything to accuse her of. Though his dislike of her was so strong, he might've just made something up in the absence of real grievances.

There was still the matter of the letters. Julian hadn't written them. Neither had Benetta. It was entirely possible Mr. Globe, or maybe even his snotty assistant, had, but Lillie didn't think that fit.

She glanced at the clock. Mr. Abora would be revealing his grand plan in the next hour or so, then everyone at the town hall would be...well, not satisfied, but they'd have their answer. Mr. Globe would get richer from the influx of new tenants, and the town would start humming again. Maybe Wineke and her partner could take over the bakery from Lillie. Despite their harsh words, Lillie liked Wineke.

"Oh, good, you're back! I've got some juicy gossip," Rey said, appearing in his mousehole.

"And I've got gossip for you, too," Lillie said.

"Well, let's start with mine, because some of it's about you," he said. "Did you know that Julian Globe has been telling people to avoid your bakery because you're putting magic into your goods?"

"Yes, actually," Lillie said with a sad smile. "That's the gossip I was going to share with you."

"Ah, well, drat." He deflated. "That was the most interesting thing I found. The other's about the folks at the town hall."

Lillie sat up. "What about them?"

"Well, it turns out that they're all about to get their property back," Rey said. "Rather anticlimactic to the entire episode if you ask me."

"What are you talking about?" Lillie said.

"Per the new laws pushed out from King's Capital, magical creatures are allowed to reclaim any land they once held *or* should be adequately compensated by the current owner."

Lillie blinked. "What does that mean?"

"Well, in terms of Benetta Pearlson," Rey said. "She has every right to get her property back. And Mr. Globe, who's been collecting rent all these years, will have to pay her the amount he collected during the time he unfairly claimed ownership of the property."

Lillie let out a noise. "He's going to hate that. I wonder if Mr. Abora's told him."

"Oh, he and Mr. Abora knew about that ages ago," Rey said. "Lenoire at the inn—she hears all the scuttlebutt—she told me they'd had a long discussion about it weeks ago."

"W-weeks ago?" Lillie blinked.

"They met again last night, very late. Lenoire didn't hear what they discussed. Probably Kemp softening the blow to the old merchant. He's going to lay an egg when he has to pay all that money to the newly-returned." He chuckled. "Can you imagine? He thought he could swoop in and steal all the property for himself. Now he's gonna pay for it. I'm sure he's got the money stashed away, but—"

"That's not..." Lillie narrowed her eyes, recalling a conversation with Benetta a few days ago. "Mr. Abora's telling the newly-returned that he can find them another spot owned by Mr. Globe. There's been no talk of just...giving the property back. In fact, Benetta was hoping to pressure Mr. Kemp into doing just that, but it didn't sound like he was budging." Lillie sat back. "So he's been lying to us about it?"

"Well, he does work for Mr. Globe."

"No, he's the assistant mayor," Lillie said. "He works for the town of Silverkeep. For Mayor Robinson."

"Oh, Mayor Robinson isn't real," Rey said, as if that were common knowledge. "Mr. Globe told everyone he was the mayor, but he doesn't exist."

Lillie blinked. "The mayor doesn't exist? How is that even possible? The queen's election monitors were sticklers for rule-following. I doubt even Mr. Globe could've pulled the wool over their eyes."

"Well, he was running unopposed these last six years," Rey said with a chuckle. "And I'm sure if anyone had a wild hair to throw their hat in, Mr. Globe would have *strongly* suggested otherwise. After all, he's the de facto mayor. Mr. Abora works for him and does his bidding." He tilted his head. "I'm surprised that's not common knowledge in the bigger community."

Lillie put her hands on her hips, thinking back to her conversations with Mr. Abora. He'd told her he was worried about fairness, and doing the right thing by everyone, but what if that wasn't his end goal? What if it was preserving Mr. Globe's wealth and status as the man who controlled everything? After all, if he was no longer everyone's landlord, he could no longer pressure them to do his bidding.

"So Mr. Abora is lying to the newly-returned,

telling them they have no claim to their property, when in fact, his boss Mr. Globe is the one without a claim. He's protecting Mr. Globe."

"Much like Mr. Globe charging you and the Kovens when he had no right to," Rey said. "Oh, Lillie, this is quite the scandal."

"I've got to talk with Mr. Abora. Surely, there's some kind of misunderstanding," Lillie said. "Or maybe I can talk some sense into him about what's right and wrong. He seems like such a nice man." She rose, looking around the bakery. "And if that fails, maybe I'll inform the masses of the new laws myself. After all, Julian Globe already told the town to avoid the bakery. What else can they do to me?"

Chapter Twenty One

Palms sweaty, Lillie walked to the town square, but instead of heading to the town hall, she made a left toward the Silverkeep Inn. Noemi was at her post, reading a book, and looked up with a scowl when Lillie walked in.

"What do you want? Here to poison me like you almost did to Benetta Pearlson?"

Lillie forced a smile. "Did you know Julian Globe ate cookies from my trash to find that out? They weren't going to be served to anyone."

She shifted. "There was jam on my floor, too."

"Goodness gracious." Lillie rolled her eyes.

"Well, you and Julian can enjoy eating jam off the floor and discarded cookies out of my compost pile if you like, but I want to speak to Mr. Abora."

"I have no idea where he is—"

"I know that Mr. Globe and Mr. Abora are lying about who really owns the property," Lillie said. "And there's *probably* an innkeeper sitting at the town hall who's keen to get their inn back, so my guess is, you also know that you have no claim to this property."

"I don't own it," Noemi said. "I manage it for Mr. Globe."

"Well, then." Lillie shrugged. "You should have no problem pointing me in Mr. Abora's direction."

Noemi surveyed her for a long moment then thumbed toward the kitchen. "Back there."

"Thank you very much."

Lillie passed the innkeeper, wondering *why* the citizens of Silverkeep liked to eat things out of the trash, and headed into the kitchen. There she found Mr. Abora, looking harried and like he hadn't slept in days. Pages of half-written papers were spread out over the entire table, with what appeared to be the names and addresses of everyone in Silverkeep.

"Noemi, I said don't disturb me until…" He locked eyes with Lillie and exhaled. "Oh, Ms. Dean. The town meeting isn't until ten."

"Yes," Lillie said. "Quite full over there. I brought a cake, but I doubt anyone will want to try it after Julian Globe spread a rumor that I was controlling everyone's minds with chocolate."

"Mm." He swapped papers around then swapped them again. "I'm terribly sorry, but I can't chat. I still haven't gotten this plan sorted in a way that makes sense."

"I don't—"

Lillie picked up a nearby piece of paper, her mouth falling open. The handwriting was identical to the letter she and the Kovens had received. She looked up at Mr. Abora, who'd gone back to focusing on the papers in front of him, then pursed her lips in anger.

"It was you?" she asked, betrayal and anger rising up within her.

"Ah, there's the Randolphsons," Mr. Abora said, snatching the paper out of Lillie's hand and ignoring her question. "Great, I can put them... Well, I don't know. They only had their shop five years before the war—"

Lillie crossed her arms over her chest. "You do know that everyone who *owned* property before the war is entitled to reclaim it, right? Per the king's law."

Mr. Abora finally looked up again. "We're still waiting on—"

"No, you're not," Lillie said. "You've known about the laws for weeks, and you've been dragging your feet on telling people because you don't want your boss to lose any money."

He avoided her gaze. "I'm not sure I know what you're talking about. And I really need to come up with a plan in the next...fifty-seven minutes or else the town is going to eat me—"

"The plan is: Benetta and the Slooses and everyone else who owned property gets it back. And Mr. Globe has to give up the property, remove his tenants, *and* pay the rightful owners the rent he unfairly collected in their name." Lillie narrowed her gaze. "Which begs the question... Why in the *world* did you write me a nasty letter and tell me to leave?"

"I didn't... I don't..." Mr. Abora twitched nervously.

"The handwriting," Lillie said, pointing to the paper. "Come now, Mr. Abora. Tell me what's going on. What in the world are you doing?"

"I don't *know*!" He collapsed onto the table, his head in his hands. "Oh, Lillie, it's such a mess. Everything is a mess! Mr. Globe is about to have my head. He told me to get the rightful owners to sign new lease agreements with *him* as quickly as possible so they'd be locked in to paying him rent, but none of them would. So I thought, if they could at least move back into their old properties, maybe they'd be willing to sign, and the only way to do that anonymously was..." He shook his head. "I thought it was kind."

"By making us all worry?" Lillie asked.

"The transplants, the ones who'd agreed to move after the purge, they all had some awful thing they were trying to run from." He sniffed. "Scandals, bad debts, that sort of thing."

"Like Maire," Lillie said. "Did you write letters to all the transplants?"

He nodded. "Everyone I had leverage on. But none of them were swayed. Everyone just kept digging their heels in deeper." He swallowed hard. "I don't even know what to do."

"Wait, then why did the Kovens and I get one?" Lillie asked. "We're not at the town square. Nobody wants our property back."

He let out another deep, shamed sigh. "I knew Mr. Moussison really owned that property, and I knew he'd never left. The Kovens had been paying Mr. Globe even though they didn't have to. So... Well, I wanted both of you to leave before anyone found out about *that*."

"You've been letting those sweet fisherfolk pay two gold coins to Mr. Globe all this time?" Lillie asked.

"Mr. Globe can be...persuasive. It wasn't such a stretch to think a small mouse wasn't the real landlord," Mr. Abora said. "I know it was wrong, but what was I to do?"

"The right thing," Lillie offered. "And speaking of that... How in the world did you know about what I did in Lower Pigsend?"

"Truth be told," he said with a furtive look, "I don't know exactly *what* you did. Back when I was staying at the Weary Dragon, I overheard you talking with Bev about a mistake you'd made in Lower Pigsend. I hoped mentioning it might've been enough to convince you to...well, leave."

"But you told me to come," Lillie said. "I wrote to you and asked if you still had space for me. You said you did."

"The day you arrived, so did the first folks from Lower Silverkeep," Mr. Abora said sheepishly. "And as for why Mr. Globe wanted you, he wants Julian to give up the bakery. Thought if there was a rival baker here, he might get the hint."

"Yeah, well, Julian certainly made sure no one would come to my bakery, didn't he?" Lillie said.

"For what it's worth, I'm sorry. Anonymous letters seemed like a kinder way to... Well, no one would get..." He fumbled over his words. "It didn't work, though. I've got a town full of people who all want the same thing, and a very scary boss who'll flip his lid if I don't make everything exactly as he likes it."

"You don't have to work for Mr. Globe, Kemp," Lillie said gently.

He looked up at her. "What? Of course I do, he pays my salary. And he owns the apartment I live in—"

"Does he?" Lillie tilted her head. "Or does one

of the people at the town hall?"

Mr. Abora opened and closed his mouth.

"I know there's no Mayor Robinson, either," Lillie said. "Not sure how you got that one past Petula Banks—"

"It wasn't easy." He shivered.

"But the point is, you're the closest thing Silverkeep has to a real mayor. So that means you need to do what's best for the *town*, not one very rich man. The right thing is what the king has decreed. Besides that, it's only a matter of time before someone from King's Capital comes and sets it all right."

He nodded. "Mr. Globe wasn't convinced that was happening any time soon, and that's why he… well…" His shoulders drooped and he put his head down on the table. "I don't know how I'm going to get out of this one."

"Come on." Lillie pulled him back upright. "Everyone already thinks I'm a monster. Why don't I go with you to share the bad news? Or good news, depending on who you are." She shrugged. "Happy to be the bad guy one more time."

Lillie and Mr. Abora walked the short distance back to the town hall, with Lillie all but dragging the nervous assistant mayor. He hemmed and hawed, offering all kinds of excuses (and gold) if Lillie would forget the whole thing. But she kept walking, intent on spilling the beans with or without him.

She opened the doors to the town hall, finding it even *fuller* than it had been when she'd dropped off the cake. She walked the length of the room, aware that she was the central focus of everyone in the room—or rather, Mr. Abora was, as he scurried behind her. She only stumbled once when she spotted Mr. Globe sitting on a bench in front, and Julian, who'd clearly been in the middle of baking as he still wore his stained and smeared apron, beside him. The elder Globe glared at Lillie as if he knew what was coming, while the son kept his gaze averted.

Good. He should feel awful for what he did.

Lillie all but yanked Mr. Abora behind the table, turning to the crowd and realizing with a start that it was *much* larger than she'd anticipated. She'd never spoken in front of a crowd like this, and started to wonder how Bev managed it all those times back in Pigsend.

"I-I..." Lillie started. "Mr. Abora, why don't you start things off for us?"

"Erm, yes." Mr. Abora cleared his throat, his gaze sliding to his boss. "T-thank you all for coming. I'm s-so glad that w-we could—"

"Enough with it!" Benetta barked from the crowd. "Tell us the plan. Do we get our property back or not—"

"Well, I'm getting to that—"

"Hurry up then!" Maire stood up. "Because if you think I can stay in this room with these *monsters* one more second, you're joking."

"Monsters?" Benetta cried, jumping to *her* feet. "We are victims of an unjust queen and her overzealous soldiers! All we want is to reclaim our lives and our property—"

"That property doesn't belong to you. You gave it up." Maire shot back. "Meanwhile, we've been here growing the town and keeping it afloat while you've been who-knows-where—"

"Ladies, please," Mr. Abora tried, but his voice was so quiet and meek no one seemed to hear it.

"These transplants you've brought to town are the monsters," Greeley said, jumping to his feet. "Starting with *that* one!" He pointed at Lillie.

A woman with curly orange hair jumped to *her* feet and pointed at Greeley. "You're one to talk! Walking into *my* apothecary and demanding I leave! Do you even know how much work I put into it?"

Lillie put her fingers to her lips and whistled loudly, catching everyone's attention. "Okay, that is *enough*. All of you. Sit down." She glared at Benetta, who glared back. "Sit down, or I won't tell you what the plan is."

With a scowl, the seamstress plopped down.

"Look." Lillie ran a hand over her curls, "I know the world is upside down. Goodness knows that none of us expected the queen to show up six years ago. Nor did we expect her to be as heavy-handed as she was. Now, we're faced with another reset, with the king back in power. It hasn't been easy for any of us, and I can absolutely understand the fear and worry. But that doesn't mean we have to be at each other's throats, does it?"

No one looked swayed.

"It's like these cakes," Lillie said, gesturing to Julian's and hers that still sat, untouched, on the table. "I certainly didn't expect Julian to bring one. Nor did he expect me to bring mine. But here we are. Two cakes. And we have a crowd full of hungry people. That seems like a win-win situation to me. Everyone can have more cake." She gestured toward the door. "Down by my bakery, there are tons of shops without an owner. Plenty of apartments without tenants. Looking out at all the people here, I know some of you would be happy down there."

"Nobody goes to the wharf," Maire said plainly.

"People would go there if they lived there," Lillie said. "When I moved into my bakery, I thought it would be a chance to revitalize what was clearly an abandoned part of town. I think there are enough people to fill both places."

"Just one problem," Benetta said. "My property is *mine*."

"You're right," Lillie said, looking at Mr. Abora. "Which is what we're here to announce."

Mr. Globe changed the cross on his legs and narrowed his eyes. But he wasn't looking at her; he was looking at Mr. Abora.

"I heard from my friends back in Pigsend," Lillie said, hoping to give Mr. Abora an out so he wouldn't be in quite so much hot water. "The king's new decree is that all property should revert to the original property owners."

At once, a cheer rose from one side of the room, and the rest let out wails of upset. Mr. Globe's face grew even angrier as his upper lip curled. Lillie once again put her fingers to her lips and whistled. This time it took two or three tries to get the clamor to end.

"Thank you," she said. "Look, I know it's not what some of you wanted to hear. But I think this is an opportunity. The folks with property rights, do you really want to be back on the square? Is it that important to uproot the people who've been there, or would you be willing to start fresh near me down at the wharf?"

"I want my shop back," Benetta said, unsurprisingly.

But the rest of the room looked at each other, uncertain. "What would the rent be?" Greeley asked.

"N-no rent," Mr. Abora said, his voice quivering with the confidence he didn't have. "We would j-just transfer ownership." Mr. Globe's nostrils flared, but the assistant mayor kept talking. "If you owned a whole building, we'd find you a whole building. If you owned a shop and apartment, we'll get that. One for one." He licked his lips, glancing at Lillie.

She smiled back, feeling more confident. "So how about it? Who wants to move? Who's willing to start fresh with me at the wharf?"

No one moved, and Lillie realized perhaps too late that advertising to be near *her* bakery might not have been the best way to entice people.

But to her *ultimate* surprise, *Julian* Globe rose from his seat, crossed the room, and pulled a dull knife from his apron. He bypassed his own cake, sliding the cutter into the bottom tier of Lillie's and pulled himself a slice. He turned to the room, perhaps so everyone would see, and took a bite.

Immediately, his eyes widened. "That is...the most amazing thing I've ever had in my life. W- what did you...?" He stopped, perhaps deciding better. "I think anyone would be overjoyed to be your neighbor. And I, for one, am *happy* to have you in Silverkeep."

He continued savoring the cake as he walked back to his father, who was downright glowering at his smug son.

"I want a slice, too!" Wineke popped up, ignoring the protests of her partner. "I don't care if it has mind control. And I want to open our apothecary shop next door to the Pobyd Perfections

Bakery!"

She rushed up, taking a much larger slice from Lillie's cake than Julian had then winked at Lillie and walked happily back to her chair.

A man Lillie had never seen before, who appeared to be dressed like a merchant, rose. "I'll move my office. I'm down at the wharf all day anyway, and I'm tired of traipsing up that hill at the end of a long day."

Evangeline Jacob rose. Lillie hadn't even seen her, but she remembered the other woman had said she lived farther away from the wharf. "We'll move, too. The boys already smell of fish when they come home. Might as well make their walk shorter." She approached the table. "And I do need to come by more often for cake. The boys couldn't say enough about how much they liked what you made for us."

"Happy to make it whenever you like," Lillie said, her heart swelling.

"Now hang on." Mr. Globe rose from his seat. "You're both *my* tenants. I expect to be compensated for the loss of my properties and occupants."

"As it stands, you've been illegally collecting rents on properties you didn't own for the past six years," Lillie said, earning a wince from Mr. Abora. "And as I understand it, you actually *owe* money to the rightful owners."

A muscle twitched in Mr. Globe's jaw, and Mr. Abora let out a small whimper. Lillie hoped Mr.

Abora's bravery held when Mr. Globe got him alone. But she had a sinking suspicion the merchant would strong-arm the assistant mayor into whatever solution benefited him the best.

But the tension in the room had loosened. When faced with getting exactly what they had, the question the citizens of Silverkeep now faced was how much importance they placed on the building and location. Some, like Benetta, were clearly attached. But more than Lillie would've guessed were willing to take her up on her offer. Mr. Abora had grabbed new sheets of paper from his office, writing their names down and promising to come up with a suitable location near the wharf.

"And you're sure we won't have this problem again?" Evangeline asked Mr. Abora while she was munching on a second slice of lemon cake. "Someone coming out of the woodwork claiming their property."

"Oh, I—" He turned to Lillie. "That's a good point."

"I've got someone looking into that," Lillie said. "Let me head back to the bakery and see what he's found."

Chapter Twenty Two

Rey's Mouse Whisper Network came through, and within two days, Lillie had a list of buildings near the wharf that were definitely abandoned. There might've been more, but Rey hadn't heard for sure about the fate of the prior owner. Still, they both had a moment of silence as they compiled the list. Lillie once again considered how devastating the queen's wrath had been for the magical set then put that aside. Silverkeep was about to enter a new era, and looking forward was the only way not to drown in the sadness of the past.

As soon as the list was delivered to Mr. Abora,

he made quick work of divvying up the buildings. After the town hall, more of the newly-returned had opted to take him up on his offer to own property down by the wharf. So every day, Lillie's shop became more and more full with new faces eager to get a treat before they started the hard work of renovation.

Wineke was a frequent customer, coming for a morning *and* afternoon snack. She and Greeley took up residence in the shop next door, as well as the single apartment above. Greeley hadn't quite made it over, with Wineke explaining he still wasn't sure about Lillie's pobyd abilities, even though he was a potion-maker himself.

"You know when someone gets an idea in their head," she explained over her second blueberry muffin of the day. "But he agreed to live next door, so I'm sure he'll get over it soon. The rest of the town certainly has."

That was very true. In addition to the steady stream of customers, Lillie also had several larger orders. The lemon cake had been a resounding success, and she had three merchants asking her to make a smaller version for various events in the next few weeks. She also had five orders for solstice pies, and she *almost* had Evangeline Jacob down for a dozen weekly muffins, but she was still on the fence if she wanted to commit, or for how long.

But Lillie was happy. To boot, she'd *finally*

gotten the nerve to write a letter to her dear ones back in Pigsend. And that morning, she'd gotten a letter back.

Dearest Lillie,

I'm so happy to hear you've taken all the excitement with you to Silverkeep. Pigsend has been delightfully dull, which is how I prefer it, to be honest. Earl and Etheldra made it back safely, and they both seemed quite sad to have left you. I'll pass along your love and good wishes to them and to Merv. He's been inconsolable since you left, but that also might be because he's having to entertain a steady stream of visitors to and from Lower Pigsend through his living room.

Allen is doing all right. Vicky sent back his engagement ring and said she'd met someone she'd like to pursue a relationship with, and that hit him pretty hard. But as you well know, it's best for the young folks to spread their wings and see what else is out there. I'm hoping a nice young lady will venture through town and catch his eye, but none yet.

I'm delighted that you've settled in your new home, and that you're able to use your incredible magic and good sense to make life better for your new friends. You are a good person, Lillie Dean, and I'm very proud of you.

All my love,
Bev

PS: Biscuit says hi, too!

Lillie kept the letter in her kitchen, reading it and crying about it more times than was probably necessary. But Bev being proud of her meant more than she could put into words, and made her even more determined to make the most of her new life in Silverkeep.

Rey, of course, was beyond excited about Lillie's newfound success, and had started a list of things he wanted to learn how to bake.

"I don't know how I'm going to get chocolate chips that small, Rey," Lillie said, as she worked on batter for strawberry cupcakes. "But we can try it."

"I can saw pieces off that chocolate bar," Rey replied, chewing on the edge of a blueberry scone. "The problem's really going to be in getting these blueberries down to a manageable size."

"Yeah, they don't do so well when you chop them, do they?" Lillie said. "I'll think about it."

The bell in the front rang.

"Be right back," Lillie said with a smile to Rey as she untied her apron. She'd gotten used to being interrupted all day, and rather enjoyed it—especially as it came with money. But when she walked out into the front room, she almost tripped over her feet.

Julian Globe stood awkwardly in the front, with one of the three young women who'd been *so* excited about Lillie's chocolate chip cookies on his arm. She was practically bouncing on her feet, while Julian looked like he'd rather be anywhere else.

"Oh, hello," Lillie said, unsure why the sight of them touching disappointed her. "Welcome back. And, erm, welcome, Julian."

"I'm *so* sorry it took me forever to come back," the young woman said, leaving Julian to rush up to the case. "My father forbade it. But Julian said he'd take the hit if he found out."

"He's already on the verge of disowning me. What's one more strike against me?" Julian said.

"Wait…" Lillie did a double take. They shared the same dark skin and features, but the girl was a bright ray of sunshine to Julian's dour raincloud. "This is your sister?"

"Yes, my name's Odetta Globe," she said. "The other two with me were Inez and Wendy. They're a bit too scared of my father to cross him. But they work for him, so…"

"I see," Lillie said slowly. "When you came down here the first time…?"

"She didn't tell anyone, of course," Julian said with a glare at the back of his sister's head. "Though I should've known better. She can never say no to chocolate. It's part of why…" His cheeks grew darker. "Anyway."

Lillie leaned on the display case and gestured to the pastries inside, all of which had been freshly baked that morning. "Well, Julian, I'm glad you and your sister decided to risk it. Please, let me know what I can get you." She gave him a serious look as her upper lip twitched. "I could…always throw the cookies in the trash first, if that would suit."

He scowled as Odetta gave him a confused look. "That's not funny," he said. "I was seriously concerned—"

"You were being a nosy nelly," Lillie said. "Next time, ask. But if you want to see what I do most often with magic." She picked up a chocolate chip cookie. "Warm up and taste *divine*."

The chocolate melted, and the cookie softened. Lillie handed it over to Julian, who retracted a bit. "It's hot!"

"Oh, you big baby, it's *warm*," Odetta said, taking it instead. "And we'll take a dozen, thanks."

"So you can…make things warm again?" he

asked. "And encourage them to taste better?"

"Chocolate, butter, and sugar *need* no encouragement," Lillie said. "But it does help to goad the flour and eggs a little. Go on, take a bite. I promise it won't make you reveal your deepest truths."

He broke off a piece and took a bite, letting out a guttural sigh and shaking his head. "I've *never* made anything that tastes like this. There's no way I can compete with you."

"That's not true," Lillie said.

"No, it's true, brother," Odetta said, giving him the look only little sisters give their older siblings. "You should pack it in. There's no way you're ever going to make anything—"

"Okay, okay." Lillie held up her hands in surrender. "Why don't I get these boxed up for you? That way you can escape without anyone noticing."

She ducked into the back to look for more boxes, and when she looked up, Julian stood in the kitchen. For such a tall, well-built man, he looked rather small in her kitchen.

"Are you going to thank me?" he asked.

"For what? Ruining my reputation or saving it?" Lillie asked, folding the box on the table. "But I do think my impassioned speech about cake helped move things along."

"My father's not the sort of man I aspire to emulate," Julian said. "He's cruel. The only thing he cares about is that people bow down to his will. He's never forgiven me for *not* coming to work for him, and he'll do everything in his power to make my bakery fail."

"Including inviting a pobyd to town," Lillie said. "So why did he give you the money to start it?"

"Because he thought I'd own it, the way he owns things, not actually work in it." He snorted. "That's beneath a Globe, in his opinion. More efficient to hire it out and reap the rewards yourself. That's how he built his shipping business. He's not the one sailing the ships or making the deals. He's just...*facilitating* all of it."

"I suppose I can see the difference," Lillie said slowly. "But what do you want to do?"

"I love baking," he said, a little sadly. "I wanted to go to culinary school, but my father wouldn't hear of it. So I dutifully went to business school, but when I graduated, I didn't want to come home. I started working in a bakery and..." His eyes lit up in a way she'd never seen before. "It was amazing. But I only worked there for three weeks before my father showed up. I told him he couldn't bribe me anymore—I was paying my own way now. So he said he'd give me money to start a café if I'd come back to Silverkeep."

"Ah," Lillie said with a nod. Now it was starting to make sense. "With the assumption you'd own it, not work in it?"

"He didn't say that explicitly—an odd oversight on his part, considering he's so savvy at business," Julian said. "But now that it's been a few years, he's been hinting that I should take over the merchant business. I'm his eldest child, so I'm the one who should be running Globe Merchant Services when he retires."

"Not your sister?" Lillie asked.

"She's..." He sighed. "Her heart is too good for business, in my opinion. Neither of us have our father's cutthroat instincts, thank goodness."

Lillie could certainly see his affection for her.

"I think I could make a real go at the bakery, but with you..." He sighed. "You're going to put me out of business, Lillie."

Something about the way he said her name made her shiver. "Now that's not a positive outlook, is it? I think a better course of action is for you to improve."

"Improve at...?"

"Baking, silly." Lillie put her hand on her hip. "I could teach you."

He stared at her. "What?"

"Only if you wanted. You could join me early in the morning—I get going around four," Lillie said. "We could bake one or two things, and you could... learn from me. Enough to take it back to your café. Then we could coexist. Two amazing bakers with plenty of mouths to feed."

"You'd do that?" Julian asked. "After I've been so..."

"The innkeeper at the Weary Dragon Inn, back in Pigsend, gave me a second chance when I probably didn't deserve it," Lillie said. "So who am I to do any less?" She straightened her shoulders. "We can start with that sorry excuse for a custard."

"What do you mean?" Julian frowned.

"It's scrambled, Julian," Lillie said with a laugh. "Your first lesson is this: lower the temperature on the milk and sugar before you add the eggs. You want low and slow with custard."

He started to glare at her but seemed to think better of it. "Thank you. I may... I may take you up on those lessons. As long as no one knows."

"Don't worry. I'm *very* good at keeping secrets," Lillie said with a smile. "Now why don't you grab another two cookies from the case, because I'm *pretty* sure your sister has eaten the dozen she bought." She winked. "On the house."

As the sun cast orange rays on the shops across the street—which had all had their boards and coverings removed—Lillie pulled off her apron for the day. The rosemary bread dough had been stretched and folded and was ready for its long proof. There was a smattering of remaining goods in the displays, though Odetta Globe had ensured there was nary a chocolate chip cookie left. Julian had overpaid for them, too, insisting on giving her double the price.

Julian. Lillie smiled as she pulled off her apron. He wasn't so bad after all. She might be able to forgive him for the rumors he'd spread about her. She didn't know what the future held, but she could see one where they became friends. After all, she'd probably need to borrow more cocoa powder one day. Glad to know she had a source.

The front door opened, and Lillie walked out to greet her last customer for the day. But once again, she found herself frozen in the doorway. This time, it was the *elder* Globe who stood in her shop.

She suddenly wished Rey hadn't disappeared to visit with Lenoire.

"The bakery is looking nice," he said, walking the length of the display case. "You really are quite skilled. Kemp was right to bring you here."

"Thank you," Lillie said, trying to keep her voice even. "What can I get for you? It's the end of the day, so not much left, but I'll have more baked in the morning."

"I'm not here to partake of your confections," he said, stopping in front of her. "You've certainly done a lot with the place. Lots of work and care has gone into renovations, I see. Certainly used that advance I gave you to good use."

"It was very welcome," Lillie said, a little uneasy.

"I'm sure it was. Unfortunately, I've confirmed

that you are no longer my tenant," he said with a smile. "Who'd have thought there were such tenacious mice in Silverkeep?"

"Rey's quite the entrepreneur," Lillie said, glancing at the mousehole.

"Yes, well." He smiled humorlessly. "I was under the assumption I was moving you to town to take over one of my vacant spots and investing in your business to ensure its success. But since you're not my tenant, I'm not sure that investment was a wise one. After all, it doesn't do me any good if you're paying rent to a mouse, now does it? So I'd be well within my rights to ask for that advance back."

Lillie swallowed. She'd amassed a little bit of gold so far, but she didn't have nearly enough to repay him. Could he even demand it back? Wasn't it a gift? She really should've signed some paperwork.

"Just keep that in mind the next time you interfere with my business," he said, walking to the door. "And that includes my son."

He slammed the door behind him.

Lillie continues her adventures in

A Splash of Arcana

Pobyd Perfections Bakery

Book Two

Acknowlegments

As always, first thanks goes to my husband for believing in me and for managing the toddler in the evenings. Thanks also go to my parents, my in-laws, and my aunt for keeping the kiddos so I can keep doing what I love. Special shout-out to my writer gal-pals who keep me sane and let me brain dump when I'm stuck.

Thank you to my street team, for continuing to love these cozy books and for hyping me up when I need it.

Thanks to Chelsea, Danielle, Lisa, and Lacey for being the all-star team who make these books as amazing as they can possibly be.

Kickstarter Backers

A heartfelt thank you to the Kickstarter backers who so generously supported the series:

Sharlene Reimer, Cortney Babcock, Megan Allen, Dylan Martinez, Gabrielle Landi, The peck family, Sarah B, Ashley Stark, Katie L. Carroll, Megan "Bugaboo", Theresa Snyder, K Raine, Ceillie Simkiss, Chelsea Coates, Kate Ehrenholm, Wineke Sloos, Terry Steinke, Jim Landis, Bryan Fulton, Herman Steuernagel, Samantha Newberry, Megan Walton, Sunshinemagik, Katrina Drake, Ashley Heinzke, polinchka, Rowan Stone, Joe Monson, Boris Veytsman, Carrie Lynn Taylor, Sax is my Axe, John Idlor, Han Clarke, Marie Cardno, Rosie Pease, Marlene Renteria, Billye Herndon, Amanda Flores, Dale A Russell, Emma Adams, MichelleG, RENEE MEEKS, Ann Cofell, Stephanie Cranford, Jessica Hoyal, Natalie Munford, Amanda A Balter, David Marchetti, Gina L, pjk, Christina Baclawski, Edward Jurina, Becky B, Luso Bray, Amy Steele, Dead Fish Books, Rik Geuze, Mike Trick, Lady Ashara T, Catherine Holmes, Molly Wyatt, Genevieve

Shivers, Yngve J. K. Hestem, Crystal Palumbo, Moira Tuttle, Tianna Twyman, Tony, Taylor D, Katelyn Mason, Jessica Worgo, W.R. Gingell, Kristin Wallin, Do not want to have a name in the acknowledgements, thank you, Nora Fritsch, Rachel Green, Chloe Griffith, Claire Tang, Jasmine C, Erin L., Kayla Boss, Torradin341, Molly J Stanton, Gee Rothvoss, Amy Chadwick, Tarian Jackson, Cathleen Stout, Maggie G., Kira Bolding, Mirjam Vogt, J.S.Ruff, Rae McFarron, Stephanie Horn, Carla Bermudez, Fira Richardson, EJ Banks, Dominic Chiavassa, Naiomi, Sara Helmers, Caledonia, Mickey Spencer, Ashley Binder, Robert "MidwesternTanuki" Sroka, Suzann, Hopelessly Hannah, Astridd, Craig Hackl, JM Feathers, Craig Esser, Joanna Farris, Charlotte E. English, Elizabeth Fiedler, Jiana, Jennifer Norton, Callie Badorrek, Brock Miller, Anonymous, Mal, Jmrinkel, ArkRoTan, Josefine B., Midnightmare, Chris McGee, James Stubbs, John O., Tania Clucas, Samantha, Xiomara Reyes, CJ Evans, Catherine Banks, Debbie, Amber Armstrong, Tom and Stephanie Greeley, Brian Bauer, Brandi Causey, Hollie Dance, Kenyon Wensing, Umeki, Risa Scranton, Carolin Benzler, Corrie Pelc, K'yra, Michelle Yvon, Erin Slegaitis-Smith, Megan Iffland, Feylin, Jesper D., Rosalie Weyer, Aeryn S., Barbara, Elizabeth Sisley, Stacie Helm, Erika, Katalin Laczina, Tanner Harding,

Brittani Hubbard, Kimberly Chelf, Nava Starling, Eric R. Asher, Sean Dooley, Justin Burgess, Kathy Pompeo, Zephyr Mini, Kelly Scriven, Vander Sonder, Eriko, Mel Moore, I don't need my name in acknowledgments, Angelica Molly, Dani Hoots, Samara Lipman, Lynnsie Diamond, Toby S, Zoe Hammond, Lynne Freeman, Liz P., Juliette Reneaume, Karen Elizabeth Wrobel, Adriana Licio, Jess Irwin, Shawn Adair, Cyrielle, Catgirlloverwelsh, Christopher E, Laura Nelson, Antoinetta Aquila, Lisa L., Sarah Heile, Laura Roberts, Ginny Williams, Liana, Caitlin Millsaps, John "Thorrikk" Flemming, Stephen T. VanWambeck, renee, Sheila G, Rachel Shear, Thomas Roark, AK Momster, Emma Walsh, Lars Peter Rønnow Netchaef, Amanda Corbin, David Holzborn, Jen Parrack, Jamie Pedersen, Ray Lorenz, Nina, Julie McGhee, Holly Niemann, Emilia Agrafojo, Sarah Faith, Christina Simmers, 'Will It Work', Sean Bradley, Rebecca Buchanan, Lyra Sky, Ann M Lopez, Aaron Jamieson, Shannara M Stanchly

Also By The Author

THE WEARY DRAGON INN SERIES, A COZY FANTASY SERIES

Bev may not know who she was before she showed up in the quaint village of Pigsend five years ago, but that doesn't bother her much. She's made a tidy little life for herself as the proprietor of the Weary Dragon Inn, where the most notable event is when she makes her famous rosemary bread. But when earthquakes and sinkholes start appearing all over town, including near Bev's front door, she's got to put on her sleuthing hat to figure out what—or who—might be causing them before the entire town disappears.

Drinks and Sinkholes is the first book in the Weary Dragon Inn series, and is available in ebook, physical, and audiobook at your favorite retailer.

Also By The Author

THE WITCH'S COVE SERIES, A PARANORMAL COZY MYSTERY SERIES

After weeks of dodging her grandmother's calls, Jo Maelstrom gets news that she died, and her cash-strapped supernatural dive bar and marina, Witch's Cove, is now hers. But when the leader of the local mermaid clan washes up dead on the shore, Jo finds herself embroiled in the question of who and why – and does it have anything to do with her own grandmother's mysterious death?

A Mer-Murder at the Cove is the first book in the Witch's Cove Paranormal Cozy Mystery series.

Also By The Author

THE PRINCESS VIGILANTE SERIES

Brynna has been protecting her kingdom as a masked vigilante until one night, she's captured by the king's guards. Instead of arresting her, the captain tells her that her father and brother have been assassinated and she must hang up her mask and become queen.

The Princess Vigilante series is a four-book young adult epic fantasy series, perfect for fans of Throne of Glass and Graceling.

Also By The Author

EMPATH

Lauren Dailey is in break-up hell, but if you ask her she's doing just great. She hears a mysterious voice promising an easy escape from her problems and finds herself in a brand new world where she has the power to feel what others are feeling. Just one problem—there's a dragon in the mountains that happens to eat Empaths. And it might be the source of the mysterious voice tempting her deeper into her own darkness.

Empath is a stand-alone fantasy available now in eBook, Paperback, and Hardcover.

About the Author

S. Usher Evans was born and raised in Pensacola, Florida. After a decade of fighting bureaucratic battles as an IT consultant in Washington, DC, she suffered a massive quarter-life-crisis. She found fighting dragons was more fun than writing policy, so she moved back to Pensacola to write books full-time. She currently resides there with her husband and kids, and frequently can be found plotting on the beach.

For a full list of titles by S. Usher Evans, visit her website
http://www.susherevans.com/